THE LIST

Books by Mick Herron

The Oxford Series
Down Cemetery Road
The Last Voice You Hear
Why We Die
Smoke & Whispers

The Slough House Series
Slow Horses
Dead Lions
The List (a novella)
Real Tigers
Spook Street
London Rules

Other Novels
Reconstruction
Nobody Walks
This Is What Happened

THE LIST

Mick Herron

Published by
Soho Press, Inc.
853 Broadway
New York, NY 10003

Library of Congress Cataloging-in-Publication Data
Herron, Mick.
The list : a novella / Mick Herron.
Series: Slough House

ISBN 978-1-61695-745-2
eISBN 978-1-61695-641-7

1. Great Britain MI5—Officials and employees—Fiction. I. Title

PR6108.E77 L58 2015 823'.92—dc23 2015036249

Printed in the United States of America

10 9 8 7 6 5 4 3

THE LIST

Those who knew him said it was how he'd have wanted to go. Dieter Hess died in his armchair, surrounded by his books; a half-full glass of 2008 Burgundy at his elbow, a half-smoked Montecristo in the ashtray on the floor. In his lap, Yeats's *Collected*—the yellow-jacketed Macmillan edition—and in the CD tray Pärt's *Für Alina*, long hushed by the time Bachelor found the body, but its lingering silences implicit in the air, settling like dust on faded surfaces. Those who knew him said it was how he'd have wanted to go, but John Bachelor suspected Dieter would sooner have drunk more wine, read a little longer, and finished his cigar. Dieter had been sick, but he hadn't been tired of life. Out of respect, or possibly mild superstition, Bachelor waited a while in that quiet room, thinking about their relationship—professional but friendly—before nodding to himself, as if satisfied Dieter had cleared the finishing line, and calling Regent's Park. Dieter was long retired from the world of spooks, but there were protocols to be observed. When a spy passes, his cupboards need clearing out.

◆

There was a wake, though nobody called it that. Most of the attendees had never known Dieter Hess, or the world he'd moved in as an Active; they rode desks at Regent's Park, and his death was simply an excuse for a drink and a little stress relief. If they had to come over pious at the name of a dead German who'd fed them titbits in the Old Days—which were either Good or Bad, depending on the speaker—that was fine. So as the evening wore on the gathering split into two, the larger group issuing regular gales of laughter and ordering ever more idiosyncratic rounds of drinks, and the smaller huddling in a nook off the main bar and talking about Dieter, and other Actives now defunct, and quietly pickling itself in its past.

The pub was off Great Portland Street; nicely tradition-al-looking from the road, and not too buggered about inside. John Bachelor had never been here before—for reasons that probably don't need spelling out, Regent's Park had never settled on a local—but had developed affection for it over the previous two and a quarter hours. Dieter too had faded into a warm memory. In life, like many of Bachelor's charges, the old man could be prickly and demanding, but now that his complaints of not enough money and too little regard had been silenced by a heart no longer merely dicky but well and truly dicked, Bachelor had no trouble dwelling on his good points. This was a man, after all, who had risked his life for his ideals. German by birth, then East German by dint of geopolitics, Dieter Hess had supplied the Park with classified information during two dark decades, and if his product—largely to do with troop movements: Hess had worked in the Transport Ministry—had never swayed policy or scooped up hidden treasure, the man responsible deserved respect . . . Bachelor had reached that maudlin state where he was measuring his worth against those who'd gone before him, and his own career had been neither stellar nor dangerous. That his current berth was known as the milk round summed it up. John Bachelor's charges were retired assets, which is to say those who'd come in from other nations' colds; who'd served their time in that peculiar shadowland where clerical work and danger meet. Veterans of the microdot. Agents of the filing cabinet. Whatever: it had all carried the same penalty.

It had been a different world, of course, and had largely vanished when the Wall came down, which was not to say there weren't still pockets of it here and there, because friends need spying on as much as enemies. But for John Bachelor's people the Active life was over, and his role was to make sure they suffered no unwelcome intrusions, no mysterious clicks on the landline; above all, that they weren't developing a tendency to broadcast the details of their lives to anyone who cared to listen. It sometimes amused Bachelor, sometimes depressed him, that he worked for the secret service in an era where half the population aired its private life on the web. He wasn't sure the Cold War had been preferable, but it had been more dignified.

And now his rounds were shorter by one client. That was hardly surprising—nobody on his books was younger than seventy—but what happened afterwards? When all his charges expired, what happened to John Bachelor? It was a selfish question, but it needed answering. What happened when the milk round was done? Then the door opened, and a cold blast nipped round the room. Thanks for that, he thought. He was drunk enough to read significance in the ordinary. Thanks for that.

The newcomer was Diana Taverner.

He watched her pause at the larger, noisier group and say something which roused a cheer, so probably involved money behind the bar. Then she glanced his way, or his group's way.

"Oh god," groaned the soak next to him. "Here comes the ice queen."

"She can read lips," said Bachelor, trying not to move his own. They buzzed with the effort.

Taverner nodded at him, or perhaps at all of them, but it felt like at him. He'd been Dieter's handler. It seemed he was in for some line-managed compassion.

It was news to him that compassion was in her repertoire.

Diana Taverner—Lady Di—was one of the Park's Second Desks, and wielded much of the power around that edifice, and not a little of the glamour. In her early fifties, she wore her age more lightly than Bachelor; wore smarter outfits too. This wasn't difficult. He shifted on the bench seat; caught the end of his tie between finger and thumb, and rubbed. It felt insubstantial, somehow. When he looked up his neighbouring soak had vacated the area, and Lady Di was settling next to him.

"John."

". . . Diana."

Ma'am, usually. But this was not the office.

His group had fragmented, its constituent parts repairing to the bar or the gents, or just generally finding an excuse to be elsewhere. But this was a while seeping through Bachelor's consciousness, swaddled by alcohol as it was. He did not want to talk to Taverner, but she had at least arrived bearing more drink. He took the proffered glass gratefully, raised it to his lips, remembering at the last minute to say "Cheers." She didn't reply. He swallowed, set the glass down again. Tried to gauge how presentable he looked: a fool's mission. But he found himself running a hand through his hair anyway, as if that might add lustre, or bring its former colour back.

"Dieter Hess died of natural causes." Diana Taverner's voice was always precise, but there seemed extra edge in it now. More than was called for, fuddled intuition told Bachelor, at a social occasion. "Just thought you'd like to know."

It hadn't occurred to him there'd be any other explanation.

"He'd been sick for a while," he said. "Was on medication. Heart pills."

"Do you remember what?"

Of course he didn't remember what. Wouldn't remember sober, couldn't remember drunk. "Xenocyclitron?" he free-wheeled. "Or something like."

She stared.

I did say "or something like," he thought.

"When was the last time you saw him?"

"Alive?"

"Of course alive."

"Well then." He gathered thoughts. "That would be last Tuesday. I spent the afternoon with him, chatting. Or listening, mostly. He complained a lot. Well, they all do." He added this to avoid accusations of speaking ill of the dead. Speak ill of the whole bunch of them, and the dead don't feel singled out.

"Money?"

"Always money. They never have enough. Prices rising, and their income's fixed . . . I mean, is it just me, or do you ever think, it's not like they have mortgages to pay? I know they've done their bit and all, but . . ."

Even drunk, Bachelor wasn't sure he was putting his argument cogently. Also, he felt he might be coming across mean-spirited.

"Well," he amended. "Of course they've done their bit. That's why we're looking after them, right?"

He reached for his glass.

When he looked at Taverner again, her face was cold.

"He complained about money," she said.

"Yes. But they all do. Did. I mean, they still do, but he—"

"So he didn't mention an alternative source of income?"

Sobriety had never been so swift nor so unwelcome.

He said, "Ah. No. I mean—" He stopped. His tongue had swollen to twice its size, and sucked up his mouth's moisture.

"Strange that he'd keep that quiet, don't you think?"

"What happened?"

"You were his handler, John," she reminded him. "That

doesn't just mean making sure he's fed and watered, and listening to his grouses. It means checking his hide for fleas. You—"

"What happened?"

He'd just interrupted Diana Taverner in full flow. Better men had been sandblasted for less.

"Dieter had a bank account you didn't know about."

"Oh Christ."

"And there was money going into it. Not sure where from yet, because someone's gone to a lot of trouble to hide the source. But that in itself is somewhat suggestive, wouldn't you say?"

He was going to be sick. He could feel the heave gathering force. He was going to be sick. He was going to be sick.

He'd finished his drink.

Diana Taverner regarded him the way a crow regards carrion. Eventually, she picked up her glass. Bachelor craved that glass. He'd kill for its contents. He had to settle for watching her swallow from it.

She said, "It's hardly *Tinker, Tailor*, John. You wipe their noses, feed their cats, make sure they're not blowing their pensions on internet poker, and—and I really didn't think this needed emphasising—and above all, make sure they don't have bank accounts they're not telling us about. You want to take a guess as to why that's so important?"

He mumbled something about being compromised.

"That's right, John. Because if they've got secret bank accounts someone else is filling with money, it might mean they've been compromised. You know, I'm going to go out on a limb here. It very definitely certainly fucking does mean they've been compromised, which means we can't trust anything they've ever told us, and do you have any idea, John, do you have the remotest idea of the headache that'll cause? When we have to go trawling through everything we ever thought we knew about everything they ever told us? To find out where the lies start, and what actions we took based on them?"

"Ancient history," he found himself saying.

"That's right, John. Ancient history. Like discovering your house's foundations aren't made of stone but pizza dough, but what's the harm, right? Now go get me another one of these."

He did what he was told, each action muffled by a sense of impending doom. The floor buckled beneath his feet. Laughter boomed from the youngsters' table, and he knew it was aimed at him. He paid for three doubles, downed the first, and carried the survivors back to land.

Look for a loophole, he screamed inwardly. Just because this is happening doesn't mean it can't be unhappened. He was fifty-six years old. He didn't have much of a career, but he didn't have anything else going for him.

Setting her drink in front of Lady Di, he asked, "How long?"

"More than two years."

"How much?"

"Eighteen grand. Give or take."

He said, "Well, that's not—"

She raised a hand. He shut his mouth.

For a few minutes, they sat in silence. It was almost

peaceful. If this could go on forever—if there never had to be a moment when the consequences of Dieter Hess receiving money from unknown sources had to be faced—then he could live with it. Stay on this seat in this pub, with this full glass in front of him, and the future forever unreached. Except that the future was already nibbling away, because look, see, his glass, it was emptying.

At last, and possibly because she was reading his mind, Taverner said, "How old are you, John?"

It wasn't a question you asked because you wanted to know the answer. It was a question you asked because you wanted to crush your underling underfoot.

He said, "Just tell me the worst, would you? What is it, Slough House? I'll be sent to join the other screw-ups?"

"Not everyone who screws up gets to join the slow horses. Only those it'd be impolitic to sack. That clear enough for you?"

That was clear enough for him.

"Dieter was an asset," she went on. "And assets, even retired assets, even *dead* assets, fall on my desk. Which means I do not want the Dogs sniffing round this, because it makes me look bad."

The Dogs were the Service's police.

"And what makes me look bad makes you look redundant."

Her eyes had never left his during this speech. He was starting to get an inkling of how mice felt, and other little jungle residents. The kind preyed on by snakes.

"So. How do you think we resolve this situation?"

He shook his head.

"Excellent. And there's the can-do attitude that's made your career such a shining example to us all." She leaned forward. "If this gets to be an inquiry, John, you won't just be out on your ear, you'll be implicated in whatever crap Dieter Hess was up to. I'll make sure of that. And we're not just talking loss of job, John, we're talking loss of pension. Loss of any kind of benefit whatsoever. The best your future holds is a job in a supermarket, assuming you're still of working age when they let you out of prison. Just stop me when you come up with a plan. Not stopping me yet? It isn't looking good, John, is it? Not looking good at all."

He found his voice. "I can fix this."

"Really? How very very marvelous."

"I'll find out what he was doing. Put it right."

"Then I suggest you start immediately. Because that's how soon I'll expect to be hearing from you."

She put her glass down.

"Are you still here?"

He made it to the street somehow, where he went stumbling for the nearest lamp post, grabbed it like a sailor grabs a mast, and puked into the gutter, all the evening's drink pouring out of him in one ugly flood.

Across the road, a well-dressed couple averted their gaze.

It might have been the hangover, but the leakage from the headphones of the man opposite sounded like a demon's whisper. John Bachelor was on an early train to St. Albans, his limbs heavy from lack of sleep, his stomach lumpy as a punch-bag. Something pulsed behind his left eye and he was sure it glowed like a beacon in the gloomy carriage. The demon's whisper slithered in and out of meaning. Every time he thought he'd grasped its message, his mind greyed it out.

He had not had a good night. Good nights, anyway, were rare—at forty, Bachelor had discovered, you began dreaming of gravestones. After fifty, it was what you dreamed of when you were awake that frightened you most. Could Diana Taverner really engineer him behind bars? He wouldn't bet against it. If Dieter Hess had been in the pay of a foreign power, Bachelor would be guilty by default. Implicating him would be child's play to an old hand like Taverner.

The train flashed past a fox curled up in weeds by the side of the track, and two minutes later pulled into the station.

Bachelor stepped out into light rain, and trudged the familiar distance to Hess's flat.

For the past ten years he'd called here at least once a week. Two days earlier, letting himself in, he had known—was almost positive he'd known—that he'd be finding Dieter's body. Dieter had been sick for a while. Dieter had been an old man. And Dieter hadn't been answering Bachelor's calls—the fact was, Bachelor should have been there sooner. So the sight of Dieter at peace in his armchair, his passing eased by wine, tobacco and music, was, if anything, a relief. If he'd found Dieter face-down on the carpet, frantic scrabble marks showing his attempts to reach the phone, Bachelor would have had to work the scene a little, cover up any appearance of neglect. He'd been Dieter's handler, as Taverner had kept reminding him. Letting his charges die alone in pain didn't look good.

Any more than having them turn out doubles did.

But it was too soon to say whether Dieter had been a double. There were other explanations, other possibilities, for Dieter having had an illicit source of income. All Bachelor had to do was find one.

The flat had been searched, as protocol demanded, but not torn apart—the significance of the paperwork removed from Dieter's desk had only come to light back at the Park. What John Bachelor embarked on now was more thorough. He began in the kitchen, and after spreading newspaper on the floor he went through cupboards, opening jars and dumping their contents onto the paper; reading the entrails of Dieter's groceries, and finding nothing that shed light on his own future or on Dieter's past. All that came to light were coffee grounds and teabags, and surely more jars of herbs and spices than a single man could have need of? No secrets buried under packets of sausagemeat in the freezer drawers. Nothing under the sink but bottles of bleach and the usual plumbing. As he searched, Bachelor found himself working faster, intent on finishing the task in hand, and forced himself to slow down. He was breathing heavily, and on the spread-out newspaper sat a mountain of mess. He should have thought harder before launching into this. He couldn't even make himself a cup of coffee now, which would have been welcome, given the state of his head.

Bachelor closed his eyes and counted to ten. When he opened them again, nothing had improved, but he thought his heart had slowed a little. Was beating at more like its usual pace.

Think, he commanded himself. Arriving here, full of his nighttime furies, he'd gone off like a Viking, which would only have made sense if Dieter had been a Viking too. But Dieter had been an old man who'd lived a careful life. A careless one would have proved much shorter. His habits of secrecy were unlikely to be laid bare by a whirlwind uprooting of the contents of his kitchen . . . *Think*.

Leaving the mess in the kitchen, he walked through the rest of the flat.

Hess's sitting room—the room in which Bachelor had found him—was the largest, occupying as much space as the others put together. Bookshelves covered three of the four walls; against the fourth, below the window and facing inwards, was Dieter's armchair. His books were the view he appreciated most, and Bachelor had spent many afternoons listening to the old man rabbit on about their contents; sessions that had reminded him of interminable childhood Sundays in the company of his grandfather, whose mind, like his shelves, was not as well stocked as Dieter's, but whose appetite for rambling on about the past was just as insatiable. At least in Dieter's case the view backwards was panoramic. He had studied history. On his shelves was collected as much of the past as he'd been able to squeeze onto them; mostly early twentieth century, and post-war too, of course. He'd once confided to Bachelor—being a handler meant hearing all sorts of secrets: romantic, political, emotional, religious; meant hearing them and passing them on—that he nursed a fantasy of finding, in all that convoluted argy-bargy of politics and revolution, pogrom and upheaval, the key error; the single moment that could be retrospectively undone, and all the messiness of modern Europe set to rights. In Dieter's perfect world, he'd have stayed the German he was born. East and west would have been directions on a map.

Borderline obsessive, had been the verdict from the Park. But then, if your retired assets weren't borderline obsessive, they'd never have been assets in the first place.

There was poetry too, and fiction in a segregated corner, but Hess's taste in that area had been stern. He'd admired Flaubert above all writers, but had a compulsion to arrange, and rearrange, the great Russians in order of merit, as if the bulky tomes were jostling for a place in the starting line-up. Just looking at these novels' width aggravated Bachelor's headache. Their colours were as dull as their contents threatened, but a cheekier red-and-white spine nestled among its beefy brothers and sisters proved to be a paperback of Robert Harris's *Fatherland*. He wondered if that, too, had offered a glimpse of a happier twentieth century for Dieter Hess. One in which the war had fallen to the other side.

He moved on. The flat was near the railway line, and from the bathroom window could be seen trains heading for London and deeper into the commuter belt. It was a sash window and the wood had rotted round the edges of the frame, and its white paint flaked at the touch. It was about a year past the point Dieter should have had something done about it, just as the carpet—fraying around the rods holding it in place at the bathroom and kitchen doorways—was beyond shabby and edging into hazard country. It wasn't a big flat. If you tripped in a doorway, your head was going to hit something— the bath, the cooker—on its way down. Bachelor supposed he should have pointed this out back when it was likely to do some good, but the way things turned out, it hadn't mattered. He opened the bathroom cabinet, then closed it again. He wasn't looking for anything hidden in plain view.

The bedroom was small, with a single bed, and a wardrobe full of old-man shirts on wire hangers, their collars frayed. A faint smell he couldn't put a finger on brought hospitals to mind. The window overlooked the front street, and was near enough to a lamp post for the light to have been a bother. More books were stacked in piles along one wall. On a chest of drawers sat a hairbrush still clogged with old-man hair. Bachelor shuddered, as if something with a heavy tread had stomped across his future. Except even this, even this much, was going to look pretty desirable if he wound up paying the price for Dieter's secret life.

It was all neat enough. Everything where it was supposed to be. What if the only things hidden were hidden inside Dieter's head? What if there were no clues, no evidence, and the bank account was nothing more than his own savings, channeled through various offshore havens in order to, whatever, hide it from the taxman? But would Dieter have known how to do that? He'd been a bureaucrat. He'd known how to open a filing cabinet and use a dead-letter drop, and even that much had been decades ago. Money laundering would have been a whole new venture, and why would he be laundering his own money anyway? Bachelor was grasping at twigs, and knew it. He needed to stop the panicky theorising and get to work.

He was there for hours. He started over in the bathroom, prising the cabinet off the wall and shining a torch into the corners of the airing cupboard. In the bedroom he upturned the furniture and ran a hand round the skirting board, check-ing for hidden compartments. He worked the bookshelves, because he had no alternative, opening book after book, hold-ing them by the spines and shaking, half-expecting after the first few hundred that words would start floating loose; that he'd drown in alphabet soup. Halfway done he gave up and returned to the kitchen, stepped around the mess he'd made and put the kettle on, then had to rescue an untorn teabag from the pile. He drank the unsatisfactory cuppa upright, leaning against the kitchen wall, glaring at the fraying ends of the carpet where it met the rod at the doorway. And then, because he couldn't face returning to the unending bookshelves, he knelt and prised the rod up. It came away easily, as if used to such treatment, and one of its screws dropped onto the lino and rolled under the fridge. Setting the rod aside he raised the carpet. Below it was an even thinner, disintegrating underlay, part of which came away in Bachelor's hand as he tugged.

In the exposed gap, so obviously waiting for him it might as well have been addressed, lay a plain white envelope.

In a pub on a nearby corner, Bachelor took stock. It was early doors, and he was first there, so he spread the contents of the envelope on his table as he supped a pint of bitter and felt his hangover recede slightly, to be replaced by something larger, and worse. If he'd hoped for an innocent explanation for Dieter's secret bank account, these papers put the kibosh on that. Dieter hadn't been innocent. Dieter had been hiding something. Had hidden it not only in an envelope beneath his carpet, but in code.

3/81.

4/19.

5/26.

And so on . . .

There were two pages of this, the numbers grouped in random sequences: four on one line, seven on the following, and so on. Twenty lines in all. Typed, they'd have taken up less than half a sheet, but Dieter Hess had been old school, and Dieter Hess didn't own a typewriter let alone a computer. And what this was was old-school code, a book cipher. They still taught book ciphers to newbies, in the same way they still taught Morse, the idea being that when it all went to pot, the old values would see you through. A book cipher was unbreakable without the book in front of you. Alan Turing would have been reduced to guesswork. Because

there were no repetitions, no reliable frequencies hinting
that *this* meant E and *that* was a T or an S. All you had were
reference points. Without the book they were drawn from
you were not only paddleless, you didn't have a canoe. And
one thing Dieter had had in abundance was books—with
all that raw material on his shelves, he could have con-
structed a whole new language, let alone a boy-scout code.
An impossible task, thought Bachelor. Impossible. No sen-
sible place to begin.

Then he took the old man's copy of *Fatherland* from his
pocket, and deciphered the list.

Two pints later, he was on the train heading back into London.
It was mostly empty, but he could still hear that demonic
whisper—maybe it was Dieter. Maybe he was haunted by
Dieter Hess.

The list had been precisely that: a list. A list of names,
none of which meant anything to Bachelor. Four women, six
men: Mary Ableman to Hannah Weiss; Eric Goulding to
Paul Tennant. *Dum de dum de dum de dum.* Just thinking them,
they took on the rhythm of the railway. Why had Dieter
copied them out, hidden them under his carpet? Because it
was a crib sheet, Bachelor answered himself. Whoever these
people were, Dieter had referred to them often in whatever
coded messages he had sent, ciphered letters painstakingly
printed in his large looping hand. To save reciphering them
every time, he'd copied out this list. It wasn't Moscow

Rules—was shocking tradecraft—but to be fair to Dieter, he'd grown old and died before anybody stumbled on his lapse.

Dum de dum de dum de dum. It was the sound of Bachelor's own execution growing nearer. He'd gone to find proof of Dieter's innocence. What he had in his pocket proved the bastard's guilt: he'd been writing, often enough that he needed a crib sheet, to someone with a paperback of *Fatherland* to hand—*3/81* = third page, eighty-first character = M; *4/19* = A; *5/26* = R; *6/18* = Y, and so on, and so very bloody forth … Lady Di would have him flayed alive. Just knowing there were names being bandied round in code: she'd have him peeled and eaten by fish. And god only knew what she'd come up with if it turned out these coded characters were up to *mischief*.

He could abscond, the three pints of bitter suggested. He could flit home, grab his getaway kit—passport and a few appearance-adjusting tools, including fake glasses and a shoe-insert, to give him a limp: heaven help him—but even if the bitter had been convincing, the plan fell apart at the first hurdle, which was made of money. Divorce had cleaned him out, and it had been years since his escape kit had included the couple of grand that was the bare minimum for a disappearing trick. And it was one thing imagining himself a stylish expat in Lisbon, admiring the sunshine from a café on the quay; quite another to picture the probable reality: hanging round bus stations, begging for loose change.

Besides, even if he'd had the money, did he any longer have the nerve? The view through the windows was dreary, a grey parade of unidentifiable crops in boring fields, soon to be replaced by the equally unappetising back-ends of houses, with flags of St. George's hanging limply from upstairs windows, and mildewed trampolines leaning against fences—but it was where he belonged. Everyone needs somewhere to imagine escaping from, which didn't mean they wanted to leave it for good. Those young-man dreams of living each day as if it were your last, they wore off; showed up, in the cold light of after-fifty, for the magpie treasures they were. Live every day as if it were your last. So come nightfall, you'd have no job, no savings, and be bloody miles away. He wanted to stay where he was. He wanted his job to continue, his pension to remain secure. His life to continue unruffled.

Which meant he had to do something about this list before Lady Di got her hands on it.

He could destroy it, but if he did that before unravelling its meaning, he might be storing up grief to come. That was the trouble with the spying game: there were too many imponderables. But a list of names that meant nothing . . . He wouldn't know where to start.

The train ploughed on, and fields gave way to houses. Even after it came to a halt, Bachelor remained in his seat, watching without seeing the half-busy platforms. At length, he stood. He had a plan. It wasn't much of a plan, and involved a lot of luck and twice as much bullshit, but it was the best he could do at short notice.

And let's face it, he told himself as he headed for the underground. You've been coasting for years. If there's any spook left in you, let's see if he can pull this off.

◆

Bachelor was headed across the river. This wasn't as bad as it sounded. In a profession whose every activity came encrypted in jargon, this one was happily literal, and didn't betoken an over-the-Styx moment, or not yet it didn't.

Some who worked there might have taken issue with this. The office complex from which various Service Departments operated—Background, Psych Eval and Identities, among others—was far removed from the dignity of Regent's Park, and a sense of second-class citizenry permeated its walls. Had it been *just* across the river—had it enjoyed a waterside view, for instance—things might have been different, but in this case over the river meant quite some distance over; far enough to leave its more ambitious inhabitants feeling they'd bought a loser's ticket in the postcode lottery. Nevertheless, the phrase was geographical, not metaphorical, which meant that those working across the river were in better shape, linguistically and otherwise, than the denizens of Slough House, which wasn't in Slough, wasn't a house, and was where screw-up spooks were sent to make them wish they'd died.

But not everyone who screws up gets to join the slow horses. Only those it'd be impolitic to sack . . .

He'd made calls, discovered who the newbies were. In an organisation this size there was always someone who'd just walked through the door, and while the training they'd been put through was more intense than most office jobs demanded, they'd still be the easiest pickings. With three names in his head, he checked their current whereabouts with security: showing his pass, barking his requests, to forestall any inquisition into his motives. Two of the newbies were out of the building. The third, JK Coe, was hot-desking on the fourth floor, not having been assigned a permanent workstation yet.

"Thanks," Bachelor said. His card had been logged on entry, and for all he knew this exchange had been recorded, but he'd come up with something plausible, or at least not outrageous, to use if he were quizzed. *Coe. Thought I'd known his father. Turned out to be a different branch.*

Coe, when Bachelor tracked him down, looked to be early thirties or thereabouts, which was old for a recruit, but not as unusual as it had once been. "Hinterland" was a buzzword now; it was good to have recruits with hinterland, because, well, it just was—Bachelor had forgotten the argument, if he'd even been listening when he'd heard it. Somehow, the Service had evolved into the kind of organisation which most of its recruits had joined it to avoid, but that was a rant for another day. Coe, anyway: early thirties. His particular hinterland lay in the City; he'd been in banking until the profession had turned toxic, but his degree had been in psychology.

"You're Coe?"

The young man's eyes were guarded. Bachelor didn't blame him. The first few weeks in any job, you had to be on your mettle. In the Service, that went times a hundred. Most unscheduled events were official mind games—googlies bowled at newbies, to see how they'd stand up under pressure—and some were co-workers' mind-fucks, to see whether the virgin had a sense of humour. Depending on the department, this meant laughing off anything from a debagging to life-threatening harm, to show you weren't a spoilsport.

All or most of which probably went through JK Coe's head before he replied.

"Yes."

"Bachelor. John." He showed Coe his ID, which was about twenty-five generations older than Coe's own. "You're through with induction, right?"

"Yesterday."

"Good. I've a job for you."

"And you're . . ."

"From the Park. I work with Diana Taverner."

And there was the word *with* stretched far as it would go; way beyond where it might snap back in his face and lay him open to the bone.

From his pocket, he produced a sealed envelope containing the deciphered list of names. Before handing it over, he scribbled Coe's own name on the front.

"I want background on each of them, including current whereabouts. 'All significant activities,' is that still the phrase you're taught?"

"Yes, but—"

"Good, because that's what I want to hear about. All significant activities, meaning jobs, contacts, travels abroad. But I don't need to tell you your job, do I?"

"You kind of do," said Coe.

"You work here, right?"

"Psych Eval. I'm putting together a questionnaire for new recruits? Even newer ones, I mean."

A sheepish smile went with this.

"Maybe you'd like to call Lady Di, then. Explain why you're knocking her back." Bachelor produced his mobile. "I can give you her direct line."

"All I meant, no, nothing. Sure. Here." Coe took the envelope. "Am I looking for anything . . . in particular?"

"Information, Coe. Data. Background." Bachelor leaned forward, conspiratorially. The cubicle he'd found Coe in was surrounded by vacant workstations, but it was always worth making the effort. "In fact, let's say that what you've got here's a network. Deep cover. And you're looking to prove it. Ten ordinary people, and what you're after is the connection, the thread that links them. Which could be—well, you don't need me to tell you. It could be anything."

Coe's eyes had taken on a vague cast, which on a civilian might mean he was tuning out. Bachelor assumed it here meant the opposite; that Coe was drawing up a mental schedule: where he'd start, what channels he'd take. Analysts, in Bachelor's experience, were always drawing mental maps.

He wondered whether he should stress how confidential this was, but decided not to rouse the newby's suspicions. Besides, how stupid would Coe have to be to go blabbing to all and sundry?

He said, "The good news is, you've got a whole twenty-four hours."

"Is this live?" Coe asked. "I mean, is this an actual op?"

Bachelor touched a finger to his lips.

"Jesus," Coe said. He glanced around, but there was nobody in sight. "That long?"

"Banks shut at four-thirty, don't they? News flash. You don't work in a bank any more."

"It wasn't that kind of banking," Coe said. He glanced at the list in his hand, then back at Bachelor. "Where do I bring the product?"

"My number's on the sheet. Call me. Do this right, and you've a friend in Regent's Park."

"Who works with Diana Taverner," said Coe.

"Closely. Who works *closely* with Diana Taverner."

"Yes. I've heard she picks favourites."

Bachelor wondered if he'd made the right choice, a psych grad, but it was too late now.

Coe said, "I spent a night in a ditch last month, in freezing fog. Out on the Stiperstones?"

Bachelor knew the Stiperstones.

"I was told it was part of a reconnaissance exercise. Counted towards my pass rate. Turned out it was a wind-up. Left me so shagged out I nearly failed the next day's module."

Bachelor said, "We've all been there. What's your point?"

Coe looked like he had a point, and it was no doubt something to do with the kind of emotions he'd feel, or the sort of vengeance he'd hope to wreak, if it turned out that Bachelor had just handed him the desk-bound equivalent of a night in a freezing ditch.

"... Nothing."

"Good man. We'll speak tomorrow."

Bachelor left the building still with the ghost of a hangover scratching his skull. Maybe Coe would come up with something he could shield himself with when Lady Di made her next move. More likely this was a waste of time, but time was currently the only thing he had on his calendar.

It might help.

It probably wouldn't hurt.

It depended on how good JK Coe was.

How good JK Coe was was something JK Coe had been wondering himself. The complex knot of his reasons for joining the Service had tightened in his mind to the extent that rather than attempt untangling them, it was simpler to slice right through. On one side fell disillusionment with the banking profession; on the other, an interview he'd read in a Canary Wharf giveaway magazine with an Intelligence Services' recruitment officer. Like any boy, he'd once harboured fantasies of being a spy. The fact that here in grown-up life, the opportunity actually existed—that there was a number you could ring!—offered a glimmer of light in what had become, far sooner than he'd been expecting, a wearisome way of making a living.

It turned out that a psychology degree and a background in investment banking fitted Five's profile of desirable candidates.

That's what Coe had been told, anyway. It was possible they said that sort of thing a lot.

But here he was now, less than a week into fledgling status, and he'd been handed what had looked like a desk job but was rapidly becoming more intriguing. It might be, of course, that this was another set-up, and that Bachelor—if that was really his name—was even now celebrating Coe's gullibility in a nearby pub, but still: if this was a time-wasting riddle, it appeared to be one with an answer, even if that remained for the moment ungraspable as smoke.

Because the names he'd been given belonged to real people. Using the Background database, for which Coe had only ground-level clearance, but which nevertheless gave access to a lot of major record sets—utilities, census, vehicle and media licensing, health and benefits data, and all the other inescapable ways footprints are left in the social clay—he'd established possible identities for each name on Bachelor's list, and caught a glimmer, too, of a connecting thread. He thought of this in terms of a spider's web in a hedge: one moment it's there, in all its complicated functionality; the next, when you shift your perspective an inch, it's gone.

There were real people with these names, but if they made up a network, it can't have been a terribly effective one. Because almost all of them were lock-aways of one sort or another. Care homes, hospitals, prison . . . Each time he tilted his head, the perspective shifted.

The afternoon had swum away, leaching all light from the sky. Coe hadn't eaten since mid-morning, a bacon sandwich he'd been planning to trade off against lunch, but he hadn't reckoned on skipping supper too. He should call a halt now, but if he did, there was no telling he'd get any further with his task in the morning; odds-on he'd be called to account for that questionnaire he'd barely started. And this was more interesting than devising trip-up questions, and now he had his teeth in, he didn't want to let go . . .

But he needed help. Oddly, he had an idea where it might be found.

A lecture he'd attended the previous month had been given by a Regent's Park records officer. She ran a whole floor, it was whispered; ran it like a dragon runs its lair, and it was easy to see how the dragon rumour started, because she was a fearsome lady. Wheelchair-bound, with a general demeanour that just dared you to give a shit about it, she'd held her audience if not spellbound then certainly gobsmacked, through the simple expedient of giving the first student she caught drifting such a bollocking he probably still trembled when reminded of it now. In one fell swoop, the dragon-lady had resurrected several dozen bad school memories. She'd quickly been dubbed Voldemort.

Funny thing was, JK Coe had rather liked Molly Doran, who was every bit as round as she was legless, and powdered her face so thickly she might have been a circus turn. Her lecture—on information collation in a pre-digital era: *not*, she emphasised, an historical curiosity, but an in-the-field survival technique—had been brisk and intelligent, and when she'd finished by announcing that she would not be taking questions because she'd already answered any they might be capable of coming up with, it had been with the air of delivering a tiresome truth rather than playing for laughs. She had added, though, that she expected to see the more intelligent among them again, because sooner or later the more gifted would need her help.

Only JK Coe had offered the traditional round of applause once she was done, and he quit after two claps when it was clear he was on his own. He'd been relieved Doran had had her back to the class, shuffling her papers into a bag, and hadn't seen him.

Two thumbs down from his classmates then, but that was okay. Coe, the oldest in his recruitment wave, felt licensed to divert from the popular opinion. Molly Doran was—no getting round this—a "character," and having escaped a profession which prided itself on its characters, this being how it labelled those who read *The Art of War* on the tube, Coe was gratified to have come across the real thing. Already he'd heard two conflicting stories behind the loss of Doran's legs, and this too was a source of pleasure. The Service thrived on legends.

He could track down people with the bare minimum to go on, he'd proved that much today. It wasn't a stretch coming up with Molly Doran's extension number; nor was it a surprise that she was still within reach of it, down in the bowels of the Park, on the right side of the river.

Legends don't keep office hours.

Coe explained who he was.

She said, "You're the one who clapped, aren't you?"

He could see his reflection in his monitor as he heard the words, and afterwards had the strange sensation that his reflection had been observing his reaction, rather than the other way round. Certainly, it seemed to retain an unusual state of calm for one who'd just been presented with evidence of witchcraft.

She said, "All right, close your mouth. If you hadn't been the one who'd clapped, you wouldn't dare call me now."

"I'd worked that out for myself," he lied.

She asked what he wanted, and he explained about the list; not saying where he'd got it from, just that it was a puzzle he'd been presented with. Besides, he reasoned, Bachelor hadn't sworn him to secrecy.

"And what do you expect from me?"

"Something you said in your lecture," Coe said. "You said don't muck about with secondary sources—"

"I said *what*?"

"—You said don't fuck about with secondary sources if there's a primary available. And that there's always a primary available if you know where to look."

"And I'm your primary?"

"Or you can tell me who is."

"So you're expecting me to point you to someone cleverer?"

"I doubt even you could manage that."

She laughed what sounded like a smoker's laugh. Last time he'd heard anything quite like it, he been sanding off the edge of a door.

"That's right, JK. You did say JK? Not Jake?"

Some jerks get lumbered with Jason. Some saps are saddled with Kevin. But how many poor sods end up with—

"JK," he confirmed.

"That's right, JK, you ladle on the syrup. The ladies always fall for that."

He said, "In that case, I have to tell you, you've got a great set of wheels."

A silence followed, during which Coe's thoughts turned to the essential elements involved in forging a new identity: fake passport, fake social security number, fake spectacles. He'd need to shave his head, too . . .

And then she was laughing again, more like a rusty bicycle chain this time.

"You little bastard," she said.

"Sorry."

"Don't spoil it now. You little bastard."

He counted blessings until her laughter passed.

"So this list," she said at last. "This famous list. You've found a link and you want to talk to someone who might know what it means."

"If it is a link, and not just a coincidence—"

"Don't be boring. If you thought it was a coincidence, you'd not have called me."

Coe said, "They all have German connections. Some close, some not so close. But they all have connections."

"Oh Jesus," Molly Doran said. "I'm sorry, JK."

She sounded it, too.

"You can't help?"

"Just the opposite. I know exactly who you want to speak to."

"Then why so sorry?"

"Ever heard of Jackson Lamb?" she asked.

In his final years as a banker, JK Coe had grown understandably secretive about his profession. In that sense, joining the Service hadn't involved big changes—broadcasting your daily activities was frowned upon—but he still found it hard to avoid feeling himself separate from the general sway. It was ridiculous, stupid, counter-productive—being an agent, even a back-room, across-the-river agent, meant melding in—and he knew, too, that everyone felt this way, that everyone was at the centre of their own narrative. Still, he couldn't help it. Take this trip across town right now, to talk to Jackson Lamb. Standing on the tube, Coe was studying his fellow passengers, gauging their identities. There was a checklist he'd memorised, a cribsheet on how to spot a terrorist; and there was another checklist, allowing for the possibility that terrorists might have got hold of the first checklist and adapted their behaviour accordingly, and Coe had memorised this too. And he was mentally running through them, scoring his fellow travellers, when it struck him there was conceivably a checklist for spotting members of the security services, and he was doubtless ticking all the right boxes himself ... The thought made him want to giggle, which itself was on one of the checklists. But he couldn't help feeling skittish. He was still in his first week, newest of newbies, and he'd shared a clubby phonecall with Molly Doran, and was now on his way to meet Jackson Lamb.

Who definitely figured among the legends he'd been contemplating earlier.

Lamb was a former joe, an active undercover, who'd spent time on the other side of the Wall, back when there'd been a Wall. So he was definitely the man to talk to if you were looking for dodgy German connections stretching into the past—most of the folk on Bachelor's list were certified crumblies—but he was also someone who came trailing clouds of story, some of which had to be true. He'd been Charles Partner's golden boy once—Partner, last of the Cold War First Desks—but after Partner shot himself, Lamb had been hived off to the curious little annex called Slough House, which was right side of the river, but wrong side of the tracks. And there he'd remained ever since, presiding over his own little principality of screw-ups. Some of the stories said he'd been a genius spy; others that he'd blown a whole network, and was the only one who'd come back alive. Nobody Coe knew had ever laid eyes on him. Well, nobody except Molly Doran, and he couldn't really claim to know her.

He'd phoned Slough House and spoken to a woman called Standish. When he'd said he wanted to speak to Lamb, she seemed to be waiting for the punchline. So he'd explained about the list, and she'd told him Lamb didn't talk to strangers on the phone, and wasn't terribly likely to speak to him in person. But if he was prepared to head over Barbican way, she'd see what she could do.

What she could do involved opening the door for him. This was round the back, as she'd said on the phone: Slough House had a front door, but it hadn't been used in so long, she couldn't guarantee it actually worked. "Round back" was via a mildew-coated yard. There was no light, and Coe barked his shin on something unidentifiable, so was leaning against the door grimacing when it opened, and he came this close to measuring his length in a dank hallway.

"Now there's an entrance," the woman said.

"Sorry. That yard's a deathtrap."

"We don't get many visitors. Come on. He's on the top floor."

Trooping up the stairs felt like ascending to Sweeney Todd's lair. Coe didn't know what that made Catherine Standish, who'd have been a dead ringer for a woman in white—a lady with a lamp—had she worn white, or carried a lamp. But her long-sleeved dress had ruffled sleeves, and Coe believed he caught a glimpse of petticoat in the two-inch gap between its hem and the strap of her shoe. But Slough House, Jesus . . . Regent's Park was impressive—a cross between old world class and hi-tech flash—and his own across-the-river complex, if drab, was functional, and had been gutted and refitted often enough that you sensed an attempt to keep up with the times. But Slough House was time-warped, a little patch of seventies' squalor, with peeling walls and creaking stairs. The bare lightbulbs highlit patches of damp that resembled large-scale maps, as if the staircase had been designed by a wheezing cartographer. And in the corners of the stairs lurked dustballs so big they might have been nests. He wasn't sure whose nests. Didn't want to be.

On each landing a pair of office doors stood open. They were vacant and unlit, and drifting from their gloomy shadows came a mixture of odours Coe couldn't help adumbrating: coffee and stale bread, and takeaway food, and cardboard, and grief.

He thought something moved.

"Did I just see a cat?"

"No."

And up they went, up to the top floor, and a small hallway with office doors facing each other from either side. One stood open, and was lit by a couple of standard lamps; the effect wasn't exactly cosy—it remained a drably furnished office—but at least it looked like a space in which things got done. This was Standish's own, Coe assumed. Which meant that the other—

"You'd better knock."

He did.

"Who the hell's that?"

"Good luck," said Catherine Standish, and disappeared into her room, closing the door behind her.

Okay, so Coe was about to meet a Service legend. *Beard him in his den* was the phrase that came unbidden, and he raised his hand to knock again, this time while announcing his name in a pleasing, manly fashion, when the door opened without warning.

So here was Jackson Lamb.

He didn't look like a legend. He looked like a Punch cartoon of a drunk artist, in a jacket that might have been corduroy once, and another colour—it was currently brown—over a collarless white shirt. What a kinder observer might call a cravat hung round his neck, and his hair was yellowy-grey, with clumps sticking out at odd angles. More hair, much darker, could be seen poking through his shirt at stomach level. As for his face, this was rounded and jowly and blotchy; there was a slight gap between his two front teeth, visible below a snarling lip. Yes, like a caricature of an artist, and one in the grip of some creative urge or other. His eyes were heavy with suspicion.

"Who are you?"

"Ah, JK Coe—"

"Oh Christ. I've told her about letting strays in. What are you selling?"

"I'm not selling anything."

Lamb grunted. "Everybody's selling something."

He withdrew into his room, and since he did so without actually telling Coe to get lost, Coe followed.

The room's sole illumination was a lamp set upon a pile of books, which on second glance turned out to be telephone directories. In the feeble yellow light it cast, Coe could make out a desk whose most prominent ornaments were a bottle of whisky and a pair of shoes. In the shadows round the walls lurked what Coe took for filing cabinets and shelves. Blinds were drawn over the sole window, but a cracked blade hung loose, and through the gap some of the evening's dark leaked into the room, offset by tiny reflections of the traffic on Aldersgate Street, blinking in the beads of moisture hanging on the glass.

Lamb didn't so much settle into his chair as collapse into it. The noise it greeted him with was one of resigned discomfort.

"You're from over the river," Lamb said, reaching for the bottle.

"Ms. Standish told you?"

"Do I look like I've time to gossip? She didn't even tell me you were coming. But you're hardly from the Park, are you? Not unless they've widened their entry criteria." Looking up, he added, "It's a class thing. Don't worry about it."

"Lamb is easily bored," Molly Doran had said. "Play him right, and he'll bend your ear for hours. But if he's in one of his moods, forget it."

"But this is work," Coe had said. "It's Service business."

"That's sweet. I remember my first week." Doran paused. "Oh, and one other thing. Don't tell him I sent you. Got it?"

"Got it."

So here, in place of the truth, was Coe's reason for approaching Lamb:

"Everyone says you're the one to talk to."

"Everyone says that, do they?"

"You lived the life. Ran your own network, survived for years. They say—"

Lamb interrupted with a fart, then said in a plummy tone, "I do apologise. That's never happened before."

Coe said, "They say you were the best."

"I was, was I?"

"And my problem's about a network . . ."

He paused. He seemed to be always pausing. This time, he was partly waiting for permission to continue; partly wondering if Lamb was ever going to invite him to sit. But there was nowhere obvious to sit that didn't involve retreating into the shadows, and while he didn't actually believe anything untoward lurked by the walls, he was a little concerned about the floorboards. The air of rot was more pronounced than it had been on the stairs. He figured he was okay if he remained in the middle of the room.

Lamb had closed his eyes, and linked his fingers across his paunch. His feet were visible on Coe's side of the desk, and he was indeed shoeless, which perhaps accounted for some small part of the atmosphere. Lamb's recent emission hadn't helped. He grunted now, and when this didn't spur Coe on, opened an eye. "You don't need to tell me about your problem, son. I already know what your problem is."

So Doran had called him after all, Coe thought. He realised he was caught in the middle of some complicated game between this man and Molly Doran, as intricate as any courtship ritual, but that didn't matter now, because the important thing was, Lamb was going to explain the oddities in this supposed network . . .

"Your problem is, you're lying. Nobody talks about me on the other side of the river, or when they do, it's not to say how brilliant I am. It's to say I'm a fat old bastard who should have been put out to grass long ago."

"I—"

"And it's not only the lying. You'll never get anywhere in this business without lying. No, your problem's twofold. First off, as you've probably worked out for yourself already, you're no good at it."

"I was told not to tell you—"

"And second, it's me you're lying to."

All of this with just one eye open, trained on Coe. It was extraordinary, thought Coe, how much a badly dressed shoeless fat man could look like a crocodile.

"And you've no idea how cross I get when that happens."

But he was about to find out.

It was after nine when Catherine Standish entered Lamb's room again. Lamb was in his chair, eyes closed, shoeless feet propped on his wastepaper bin. A bottle of Talisker sat on his desk, a pair of thumb-greased glasses next to it. One was a quarter full, or possibly three quarters empty. The other, while not exactly clean, was at least unused.

She knew the routine, a recent parlour game of Lamb's. No point talking until she poured herself a glass. This was what passed, in his mind, for good-natured teasing.

Slough House had been empty of staff for hours, the pair of them apart. For Catherine there was always work to do, a neverending cascade of it. For Lamb, she sometimes thought, there was nowhere else to be. He had a home; might even— now here was a thought—have a family somewhere. She thought that less likely than finding intelligent life on Twitter, but still: there had to be a reason he spent so many of his waking hours here, even if a goodly fraction of those waking hours were spent asleep.

Without touching the glass she poured a slug of whisky into it, then added a pile of newspapers from the visitor's chair to the bigger pile on the floor next to it, and sat.

She said, "That wasn't very helpful."

He didn't open his eyes. "This is me you're talking to?"

"We're all part of the Service. So someone thought it would be funny to send a Daniel into your den. That doesn't mean he didn't need real information."

"I didn't object to the little bastard turning up. I objected to the little bastard trying to play me."

"Well, I think we can safely say he won't try that again."

JK Coe's departure had been precipitous, making up in speed what it lacked in dignity.

"Did you know him?"

"He's still in his first week. Refugee from banking, but he scored high on the entrance exams and—"

"Entrance exams," said Lamb. "God help us."

"I know," Catherine said. "Just give them a Double-Oh-Seven watch and drop them behind enemy lines. Never did you any harm."

"Well, we can't all be me," Lamb said reasonably. "What's his day job?"

"Psych Eval."

"For a washed-up alky, you're still plugged into the network, aren't you?"

Washed-up was right. Catherine's career, like a castaway's message, had been sealed inside a bottle and tossed overboard. Slough House was where it had beached, and in the years since she hadn't touched a drop.

The amount of booze Lamb had put away in that time would float a hippo.

"It's funny," she said. "I'm sitting here dry as a bone while you souse yourself nightly. How come I'm a drunk and you're not?"

"Drunks have blackouts," he explained kindly. "And wake up in strangers' beds. I never do that."

"When you start waking in strangers' beds, it's the strangers who ought to be worried."

"You say tomato," Lamb said obscurely. He reached for his glass, balanced it on his chest, and closed his eyes again. "Tell me about the kid's problem."

So she told him about the kid's problem. John Bachelor, one of the Park's old lags, had presented him with a list of names; find out who they are, Bachelor had said. Find out if there's a connection.

Find out if it's a network.

"Bachelor," Lamb said without opening his eyes. "Milkman, right?"

"He's on the milk round, yes."

"One of his mentals just died."

"Mentals?"

"Trust me, they're all mentals." Lamb craned his head forward, caught the rim of his glass in his teeth, and easing his head back again, allowed the contents of the glass to pour into his mouth. He swallowed, then set the glass back on his chest. "When Daniel Craig can do that," he said, "tell him to give me a ring."

"I've made a note."

"Dieter Hess," Lamb continued. "That was the bugger's name."

"Did you know him?"

"God no. I've better things to do with my time than pal around with clapped-out spooks."

It was true, Catherine thought, that you didn't get that adept at handless drinking without hours of practice.

"I know who he was, but not a joe, an asset. Worked in the Department of Transport on the other side."

When Lamb said "the other side," he always meant the Wall. For him, the Cold War had been geography as much as politics.

"He had access to classified info. Troop movements, that sort of thing. Fair play to him, it was useful stuff. How far did Coe get?"

Coe had done the basic searches and come up with a list of possibles connected by a thread: they all had links with Germany. They were offspring of immigrants, or had other family bonds; they had work connections; they'd studied the language and literature to degree level. In some cases, frequent holidays indicated an attachment to the country. It wasn't much, Coe had thought, but it wasn't something he was spinning out of fresh air. It was definitely there.

Lamb grunted. "And means the list definitely came from Hess. So what's the problem?"

"The problem is, most of those on the list are shutaways. In care homes, a lot of them. Elderly. There's one who's younger, thirty-two, and he's never been anywhere else. He's severely disabled. One's been in prison for the last decade, and isn't leaving soon. Of the whole crew, there's only one at liberty, a twenty-one-year-old girl." Lamb wasn't reacting to any of this. Hadn't even opened his eyes. "So what Coe wants to know is, what kind of network is that?"

She leaned back in her chair and waited.

After some minutes Lamb raised his empty glass, using his hand this time. He held it in her direction. Suppressing a sigh she reached for the bottle, and filled it for him. Her own still sat where she'd left it, untouched. She was trying to pretend it wasn't there. If she looked at it by accident—if it looked back—she would turn to stone.

Lamb said, "Any rumours on the late Hess?"

"There was money."

"But not huge great bucketloads, right?"

"Not from what I've heard."

And Catherine heard a lot. She had fallen far—there were those who'd argue she'd fallen further than Lamb—but the only enemy she'd made on the way was her own younger self. In her private life, she double-locked her doors. But at work she kept all channels open, and even Lamb was impressed by the range of her contacts, and their willingness to share with her.

But if she dealt in raw data, Lamb liked to build castles with it.

She said, "You have that look."

"What look?"

"That look where you're about to be clever, and I'm supposed to be amazed."

Lamb belched.

"Though I could be wrong," Catherine said.

"Coe's still slimy with afterbirth, so you can't blame him for being ignorant. But Bachelor's third-rate at best. Know him?"

"Of him."

"Best way. All being a milkman involves is wiping noses and he can't even do that. If he asked Coe to track down these people, it's because he doesn't want to do it via channels, which means he hasn't told anyone at the Park. I expect he found the list after Hess died, and has been crapping himself in case Lady Di gets wind of it. Coe doesn't know enough to work out what it means, and he's too stupid to do it himself."

"But you're not."

"You probably weren't either, before you pickled what used to be your brain. You never get those cells back, do you?"

When he asked a particularly nasty question, Lamb generally required an answer.

Catherine said, "They're usually full of information you don't want to recall anyway. If I ever struggle with your name, there's your reason." She thought for a bit. "The fact that it wasn't much money is a clue, isn't it?"

Lamb lit a cigarette.

She thought some more. Out on the street, a car honked and another honked back. Impossible to tell whether two friends had driven past each other, or one stranger had cut another up. There were times when it was similarly hard to tell what was happening in this room.

Hess had been receiving money to pay the people on this list. But the people weren't any kind of network; they were shut-ins and innocents.

She waved away smoke and said, "It's a ghost network."

"There you go. All you've ever done for the Service is type memos and boil the kettle, and even you can work it out. I despair for this generation, I really do. Bunch of Gideons."

She didn't ask.

Not being asked never bothered Jackson Lamb. "Talentless chancers riding on their family pull and the old school tie. Call me a hopeless idealist, but talent used to count for something."

Catherine stood. "Maybe we'll put that on your gravestone."

She was halfway out the door before he said, "You'll tell him all this, won't you?"

"Coe? Yes, I will."

"Another lame duck. Collect as many as you like, it won't help you fly again."

"I'm under no illusions about my future, thanks."

"Just as well. It's not clear you have one. Unless you count this place."

Catherine turned. "Thanks. And by the way, what *is* that round your neck?"

"Somebody's scarf. Found it in the kitchen." Lamb scratched the back of his neck. "There's a draught."

"Yes, keep it on. Don't want you catching cold."

She went back to her own office to ring Coe, thinking: *So that's where the tea towel went.*

Lamb finished his drink, then reached for Catherine's untouched glass. A ghost network. He didn't especially approve—in Lamb's lexicon, a joe was not to be trifled with; even an imaginary joe—but the old lag had doubtless done it for beer money, which left Lamb half-inclined to applaud. A ghost network didn't require joes. All it took was a little identity theft; enough to convince your paymasters you were nurturing the real thing: verifiable names, plausibly sympathetic to whatever cause you'd hired out to. In Hess's case, he'd scraped together a crew as near their last legs as he'd been himself, but that didn't matter, because there was no way the paymasters were ever going to get an actual sniff of them. *Too soon*, he'd have said. *Too raw. Bring them on gently.* Phrases Lamb had used himself, in the long-ago, but always for real. And what were they supposed to be passing on, Hess's phantoms? Nothing major. Gossip from the corridors of power, industrial tittle tattle, maybe hints of policy shifts; or possibly Hess had gone for something riskier, and pretended one of them was actually in the pay of the Service. Thinking about it, Lamb suspected the old boy could have made that fly. Milked John Bachelor for office gossip and passed it off as product, explaining the lack of substance everywhere else as being early yield; a thin harvest from a too-green vine, but let it grow, let it grow . . .

And it was only small sums of money.

He supped from Standish's glass. A low murmur from across

the hall told him she was on the phone, giving the lowdown to Coe, who'd doubtless be puppyishly grateful, and just like that Standish had another resource to call on. Networks everywhere . . . And who could be surprised, really, that a worn-out spook had found a way to supplement his pension? Hess had been an asset, and here was a thing about assets: you could never be sure they weren't going to turn 180 degrees. Lamb accepted that now as he had done then. He hated a traitor, but defined the breed narrowly. Assets switching pavements was part of the game. Because they were the ones doing the risky business, while their paymasters risked only papercuts.

"So no harm done," he muttered. Least of all to John Bachelor, who'd be able to pass the whole thing off as an old man's petty larceny; if, indeed, he bothered to pass anything on at all. Ghost networks were only a problem if you believed in ghosts. Bachelor probably scraped by without that superstition.

So no, no harm done.

Unless somebody does something stupid, Lamb thought, but really; what were the chances?

Information is a tart—information is anybody's. It reveals as much about those who impart it as it teaches those who hear. Because information, ever the slut, swings both ways. False information—if you know it's false—tells you half as much again as the real thing, because it tells you what the other feller thinks you don't know, while real information, the copper-bottomed truth, is worth its weight in fairy-dust. When you have a source of real information, you ought to forsake all others and snuggle down with it for good. Even though it'll never work out, because information, first, last and always, is a tart.

This much, John Bachelor knew.

So the best thing to have, he also knew, was an asset; someone deep in the enemy's bunker—and for information purposes, everyone was an enemy—passing back knowledge that the enemy thought was his alone. But even better than that was knowing the enemy had an asset inside your own bunker, and feeding him, feeding her, information that looked like the real thing, that nobody dared to poke at, but which was false as a banker's promise.

And best of all, better than anything else, was having it both ways; was having someone the enemy only thought was their asset inside your own bunker, so while your enemy thought he was feeding you mouldy crumbs and harvesting cake, the reality was the other way round.

All of this, Bachelor wanted to explain to Di Taverner before he got on to anything else, but that wasn't going to happen. For a start, she knew it all already. And for the rest, she had other things on her mind.

"They should have taken the carpets up," she said.

"He was an old man."

"Your point being?"

"Nobody was expecting this. Dieter's been—had been—defunct for years. As far as anyone knew he was sitting at home reading Yeats, and drinking himself into oblivion. Cleaning up after him was a matter of respect, that's all."

"If they'd respected him more, they'd have taken the carpets up," she said.

They were in her office in Regent's Park, and it was mid-morning, and the artificial lighting was pretending it was spring. On her desk lay the list; Dieter Hess's coded original. The copy of *Fatherland* with which Bachelor had unwrapped its secrets sat next to it.

"And these people," Taverner said—the people on the list—"they're all real?"

"They exist, but they're not a network." He'd told her this already, but it was important to emphasise the point: that Dieter Hess had not—had *not*—been running a coy little op behind Bachelor's back, but had simply been filching pennies to ease his days; to pay for his wine and his books; to ensure, god help us all, that he could turn the heating up. So Bachelor laid it out again, this information that had seeped down from Jackson Lamb to Catherine Standish; from Standish to JK Coe; from Coe to John Bachelor, and was even now being soaked up by Diana Taverner: that the people whose encoded names had been laboriously printed on that sheet of paper in most cases probably didn't know what day of the week it was, let alone that they were spies. Dieter Hess had picked their pockets, though all he had taken was their names.

"Why them in particular?"

"For their German links. He needed people the BND would believe in."

The Bundesnachrichtendienst was the German intelligence service.

"Do me the smallest of favours and don't treat me like an idiot. I meant why people in homes, in hospitals? Out of circulation?"

"Safer. He didn't want anyone who was going to make waves. You know, win the lottery or something. Get in the papers. Draw attention."

"Then what about the younger one? Why doesn't she fit the pattern?"

"He wanted a live one. Obviously."

Her eyes flashed danger. "What's obvious about it?"

"I didn't mean obvious, I just meant I've been thinking about it." Jesus. "He wanted someone he could demonstrate was live and kicking, if he needed to."

"Like when? How did this scam work? If it was a scam. The jury's still out."

"It worked on old-school principles," Bachelor said. "The kind that mean, if you've got an agent in place, you don't put them on parade. Hess was known to the BND, of course he was. He defected, after all. Ancient history, but still. So if he claimed, I don't know, regret, or willingness to make amends now the Fatherland's reunited, he'd have found a willing ear. He was a persuasive man. That's how he survived doing what he did. So anyway, he made his contact, and yes, *mea culpa, mea culpa*—I should have known he did that."

If he'd been hoping Diana Taverner would wave his guilt away, he was disappointed.

"Anyway." Moving briskly on. "Having made contact, he convinces whoever, let's call him Hans, he convinces Hans he's built up a network of people prepared to pass on whatever titbits their professional lives offer. The same kind of thing we'd be interested in ourselves. Now, I know you're going to say, 'But they're on our side—'"

Because it was his firmly held principle that when trying to seduce, you bowled the odd full toss.

"For god's sake, John. Who do you think you're talking to?"

For information purposes, everyone was an enemy.

"Sorry. So anyway, Hans takes the bait, and in return for a small amount of money, peanuts, he's acquired a string. But strictly sight unseen, of course, because he can't go round kicking tyres, can he? Not with a stable of spooks. All he can do is give thanks, open a bank account so Dieter can feed the fledglings, and sit back and wait for product."

"Which is what?"

"That's the beauty of it. Hess would've claimed to have long-term agents in place, the kind that take years of cultivation. So there's not going to be major product. Not right away. Which keeps Hans quiet and doesn't worry Dieter one jot, because by the time his debts fall due, and his agents are expected to be coughing up the proverbial fairy dust, well, he'll be dead. He knows how ill he is. He's not expecting a miracle recovery."

Diana Taverner's eyebrows were drawn to a point. Partly she was assessing Bachelor's story; partly his demeanour. He seemed to believe his tale, but then, he was invested in it— either Hess's list was the harmless petty larceny Bachelor was selling, or the old fool had really had been up to something, in which case it had been happening on Bachelor's watch. And while her warnings to him about prison time had been for effect, her other threats had been real. Taverner had a strict policy about mistakes. She was prepared to accept her subordinates made them so long as they were prepared to take the blame. She didn't like finding other people's messes on her desk. From a distance, they might look like her own.

On the other hand, surrendering the list was a point in his favour. He could have pretended he'd never found it, and worked up a legend to explain Hess's secret funds. Along with her policy on mistakes, Taverner had one on cover-ups: provided they came with full deniability, she could live with them.

He'd stopped talking.

She said, "And all this for a few extra quid."

"Don't discount it. We don't exactly bed them down in clover—"

"Don't talk to me, John. Talk to the Minister. And she can talk to the Treasury."

"Well, quite. But anyway, a few extra quid, a couple of grand a year, makes the difference to Dieter between a nice bottle of wine and a supermarket offer." Bachelor paused, having been struck by a vision of his own future. Where was he? Yes: "And besides . . . He was a game old bird. He probably enjoyed it."

"Maybe so," she said.

The moment's silence they shared was more of a wake for Dieter Hess than the evening in the pub had been.

She said, "Okay. You screwed up, which I'm not forgetting, but for the moment, no harm done. Hans'll no doubt come looking for his strays once he's sure Dieter's safely forgotten, so Hess's phantoms are on your watch list. I don't want to read about various shut-ins being smothered in their sleep when a vengeful BND spook finds he's been conned."

Bachelor didn't reply. He was staring at a fixed point in space that was either high above London or somewhere in the back of his own mind. Lady Di scowled. If anyone was going to fall prey to reverie in her office, it was her.

"Still with me?"

"There's another possibility."

"Enlighten me."

"You're right. Hans, whoever he is, will wait for the ashes to settle before he comes looking for Dieter's lost sheep. Which gives us a window of opportunity."

Lady Di leaned back. "Go on."

"This younger girl, the one Hess must have meant for show . . . What if we turn her?"

"You want to recruit her?"

"Why not? If she's suitable . . . We run the usual background checks, make sure she's not an idiot or a nutjob, but if she fits the asset profile, why not? Hans already thinks she's on his side, and she doesn't even know he exists. We'd have a ready-made double. How much of a coup is that?"

"Running an op against a friendly?"

"It wouldn't be an op as such. If Hans is planning a recruitment drive on our soil, it serves him right if he gets his fingers burnt. Don't pretend you don't like the idea."

As far as Diana Taverner was concerned, she'd pretend

whatever she liked. But she allowed the idea to percolate while she told Bachelor to leave, and he departed to float round Regent's Park, wondering whether he'd done enough to save his career.

Recruit one of Hess's phantoms . . . It had a nice circularity to it. Was the kind of scheme which could become a case study, a model for future strategists to ponder; how to seize an opportunity, turn it into a triumph. Backdoor views into other states' intelligence services were always welcome. Like having the chance to rummage through your best friend's cupboards. An opportunity you'd publicly deplore, but so long as they didn't find out about it, you were never going to pass up.

And as so often with Second-Desk decisions, it was the money tilted the balance. When the money side of it occurred to her, a slow smile spread across Diana Taverner's face; a smile that had been known to draw men her way, until they got close enough to notice that it never reached her eyes. Hans had been paying Hess to maintain his network; he'd be disappointed when he discovered nine tenths of this network was fake, but if he thought the girl was genuine, he'd continue paying her upkeep. Which meant the Park wouldn't have to. A detail that would bring her a standing ovation once she ran it past the Limitations Committee.

She had Bachelor paged, and gave him the go-ahead.

The waves were mostly froth: great fat spumes hurling themselves at the Cobb's sides, then spitting as high as they could reach before collapsing back into the roiling puddle of the sea. Again and again the waves did this, as if reminding the Cobb that, while it might have graced this harbour for hundreds of years, the sea had been around significantly longer, and would prevail in the long run.

That particular scenario wasn't troubling Hannah Weiss, however. Mostly, she was enjoying the figure she must cast to anyone watching from the quay. With a red windcheater and jeans in place of a black cloak, and her dark-blonde hair pulled into the briefest of knots at the back of her head, she was a far cry from Meryl Streep, but still: there was no denying the inherent romance in the scene. The waves splashed against the stone, and the grey sky was tinged with purple on the horizon, threatening rain later, and here she was; lingering on the stone arm Lyme extends into the sea, curled protectively round its bobbing fleet of boats.

And she was here with romantic purpose, of course. The man who had dropped into her life a mere fortnight earlier had brought her here, or perhaps summoned her was a better way of putting it; or perhaps—to be blunt—had sent her the rail ticket: first class return (big spender!), a cottage for the weekend, and he'd join her, within an hour of her arrival, on the Cobb. Sorry they couldn't travel together, but he'd explain all soonest. Clive Tremain, he was called. He wore a tie all week and polos all weekend, enjoyed country walks and well-earned pub meals after, and was going to do his damnedest to borrow a dog for this particular mini-break, so they could throw balls on a beach, and watch it jump across waves to collect them.

He'd turned up at a party two weeks earlier, an old friend of an old friend of the party-giver, and had cornered Hannah in the kitchen for an hour, hung avidly on her every word, then wooed her number out of her before mysteriously disappearing. She'd been on tenterhooks for forty-eight hours, which was her upper limit for tenterhooks, before he'd used it. Since then they'd been on three dates and he'd improved on each occasion, though had yet to make any significant moves in a bedward direction. And then came the weekend-in-Lyme-Regis idea, which struck Hannah as perfect, definitely one up on any invitation any of her girlfriends had yet received. Clive Tremain. A bit sticky-looking at first sight—sticky-looking as in, might just have a stick stuck up him—but that didn't detract from his looks. He had the air of one who'd taken orders in the past, and might not be above dishing them out in the future.

And now here he came, for this surely must be him—a man approaching the Cobb from the road. Wearing a black overcoat at which la Streep herself might not have turned her nose up, and bareheaded, and on the Cobb itself now, near enough for a pang of disappointment to reach her, because it wasn't Clive; was a much older man . . . She turned, glad she hadn't embarrassed herself with a wave, and keen to resume her solitary vigil over the sea, striking just the right attitude for the real Clive to admire, once he arrived, which he surely would do any minute.

"Ms. Weiss?"

She turned.

"Hannah, yes?"

And that was all it took for her to know that Clive Tremain wasn't coming to collect her; that Clive Tremain wasn't showing up in her life ever again. That Clive Tremain, in fact, had never existed at all.

Hannah Weiss. Born '91, parents Joe and Esme—such a lovely name John Bachelor had to say it again, for the sheer pleasure of the sound: *Esme*—*née* Klein, the rest of whose family were scattered across Germany like so many seedlings: Munich mostly, but enough of a contingent in Berlin for there always to be a cousinly bunk for Hannah to bed down in when, as so often during the noughties, she had spent summer vacations there; enjoying the feeling of being truly European, with a language under her belt, and friendly faces to speak it to. Then a degree at Exeter, a proper one: history. And then the Civil Service exam, and now a first-rung job at BIS, which John Bachelor made a bit of a production out of not being sure what it stood for: something to do with business, I'm guessing, Hannah, yes? Something clever to do with business? He was a different man today, John Bachelor, having donned handler's garb, which for Hannah he had decided meant Favourite Uncle.

"Business, Innovation and Skills."

"The department for," he said. "Well done. Very well done."

They were in a pub off Lyme's main street, the one that curled uphill in picturesque fashion, and Bachelor had already laid a world of apology at Hannah's feet for what was

obviously unforgivable—what couldn't possibly be counte-
nanced for any reason other than the one he was about to
produce—and had commenced wooing her with the best the
pub had to offer, which was a not-bad prawn risotto and a
decent Chablis. The rocky part, he hoped—if only the first
of many rocky parts—was over, because she had after all
listened to him when he'd explained that Clive wasn't going
to be able to make it actually, but that he himself would very
much like a quiet word.

Laying that snare for her—the word was honeytrap—was
risky, but Bachelor had deemed it necessary; partly to remove
her from her usual sphere, because recruitment was best done
in a neutral zone, one in which the object of desire had nobody,
nothing, to rely on but her own judgement. But it was partly,
too—though this could never be spoken—to establish a certain
willingness in advance: the object of affection was here to be
wooed, true, but the end result was already flagged up. The
atmosphere had prepped a "yes." The food was warm; the wine
was chilled. Outside, rain danced brightly on the road and
pavements and the roofs of parked cars, for the weather Hannah had watched approaching from the Cobb had arrived to
complete the scene.

He would like to buy her lunch, he had explained, to make
up for Clive's absence. And afterwards, she could head back to
London—first class—or, if she preferred, make use of the
cottage Clive had booked. Bachelor himself, he hastily added,
would not be included.

"There's something going on, isn't there?"

He could scarcely deny this.

"You're not planning on drugging me for sex or anything, are you? You don't look the type, I must say."

He was grateful for this, until she added: "Too wrecked looking, really." She'd looked back towards the sea then, and the purple-fringed cloud in the decreasing distance. "I take self-defence classes, by the way."

"Very wise," said Bachelor, who knew she didn't.

"Okay." This had been abrupt. "If that sod's not coming, you'll have to do. Buy me lunch."

Over which he asked her about herself and her family, and checked her answers against what he already knew, which was almost everything.

"And why did you stop going to Germany, actually, Hannah? Fall out with the cousins?"

"Well, I haven't stopped going," she said. "I just haven't been in a while, that's all. I was in the States one year—"

Coast to coast, Bachelor mentally supplied; a six-week road-trip with three friends from Uni. Hannah had split with her half of the male couple within days of arriving home.

"—and just been *really busy* since, but I'll certainly be going back next time I get a sniff of a chance at a decent break. They work you awfully hard, you know."

"Oh, I'm sure it'll get easier after a while."

Later, when the rain had passed over, and the sun was making a valiant attempt to regain control, they took a footpath leading

out of town, and Bachelor explained a little more of the cir-
cumstances that had brought him to her.

"So you mean . . . What, this man stole my identity?"

"In a manner of speaking."

"But he wasn't racking up huge debts or anything?"

"No, nothing like that. He was using your name and your
background, that's all, to convince some people that he had
recruited you as what we like to call an asset."

"A spy."

"Not really. Well, sort of," Bachelor amended, when he
noticed a certain shine in her eyes.

"So that's what you are too. You're a spy."

"Yes."

"And Clive too."

"Clive's not really his name."

"Will I see him again?"

"I see no reason why not," John Bachelor lied.

But there was something in her attitude that hinted that
Clive, anyway, had already been written out of her future.

"So what do I do about it?" she asked. "Do I have to give
evidence in court? Something like that?"

"Good heavens, no. Besides, he's dead now."

She nodded wisely.

"Lord, don't think that. He had a bad heart. He was unwell
for a long time. It was only afterwards that we—I—found out
what he'd been up to."

"So nobody knew."

"That's right."

"And nobody would still know—I mean, I wouldn't—if you hadn't just told me."

"That's right."

In the very best of cases, the object of affection wooed herself.

"So that means you want me to do something for you, doesn't it? I mean, you're hardly telling me all this just to keep me informed. Spies keep secrets. They don't go round blabbing them to all and sundry."

"They're certainly not supposed to," he said, thinking of JK Coe.

They were under trees, and a sudden gust of wind shook loose some hoarded rain, sprinkling their heads. This made Hannah laugh, and Bachelor had a sudden pang—when she did this, she seemed about thirteen, which was far too young to be wooed or honeytrapped; far too young to be recruited. But when her laughter stopped, the look she directed at him was old enough that he shook those thoughts away.

"You want me to make it real, don't you? To become what he pretended I was. Except you want me to do this while really being on your side."

"It's not something anyone's going to ask you to do," he said. "It's simply an idea that's been . . . floated."

As if the idea had risen out of nowhere, and was bobbing even now between them like a balloon, red as the coat she wore. She could burst it with a word. If she did, he would do nothing to attempt to change her mind. Nothing at all. He swore this to himself on everything he kept holy, if anything still bore that description. And even if his failure to recruit her swept him straight back into Lady Di's black books, he'd deal with that—even unto being cast out of Regent's Park, into the pit of unemployability that awaited a man his age, with what was effectively a blank CV—sooner than strong-arm this young woman into leading a shadow life.

Because that's what he'd been leading, these decades gone. A shadow life. Scurrying round the fringes of other people's history, ensuring that none of it ever raised its head in polite company.

She was looking up into the trees, awaiting the next shower.

John Bachelor knew enough not to say anything.

He watched her though, and marvelled again at what it must be like to be young, and know that you hadn't yet messed everything up. In Hannah's case, he thought, she'd continue looking young well into age. Bone structure counted. He might be trying to steal her soul, just as dead Dieter Hess had stolen her identity, but ultimately Hannah Weiss would hang onto everything that made her who she really was. That, too, he marvelled at, a trick he'd not managed himself.

She said, "Will it be dangerous?"

"Not like in the films."

"You don't know what kind of films I watch. I don't mean car chases and jumping out of helicopters. I mean going to prison. Being caught and locked up. That kind of dangerous."

"Sometimes," Bachelor said. "That happens sometimes. Not very often."

"And will I get training?"

"Yes. But it'll all have to be done in secret. As far as anyone knows, you'll still be the girl you always were. Woman, I mean."

"Yes. You mean woman."

She looked upwards again, as if the answer to her questions sat hidden among leaves. And then she looked at John Bachelor.

"Okay," she said.

"Okay?"

"I'll do it. I'll be your spy."

"Good," he said, and then, as if trying to convince himself, he said it again. "Good."

It was three months later that Jackson Lamb made an unaccustomed field trip. Hertfordshire was his destination: he'd received advance word of a wholesale spirits outlet going down the tubes, and had hopes of picking up a case or two of scotch at knockdown prices.

It was a long journey to make on the off-chance, so he went on a work day, and made River Cartwright drive.

"This is official business?"

"It's the secret service, Cartwright. Not everything we do is officially sanctioned."

Two hours later, with a satisfied Lamb in the back seat, and two cases of Famous Grouse in the boot, they were heading back towards the capital.

Three hours later, with a rather more disgruntled Lamb in the back seat, they were still heading back towards the capital.

"This is supposed to be a short cut?"

"I never claimed it was a short cut," River said. "I explained it was a diversion. A lorry shed its load on the—were you actually listening?"

"Blah blah motorway, blah blah road closure," Lamb said. "If I'd known it was a magical mystery tour, I might have paid attention. Where are we?"

"Just coming out of St. Albans. And you're not smoking that."

Lamb sighed. In return for River driving him, buying lunch and not having the damn radio on, Lamb had agreed not to smoke in the car, and was starting to wonder how he'd let himself be bested. "Turn in here," he said.

"A cemetery?"

"Does it have a No Smoking sign?"

River parked just beyond the stone gateway.

Lamb got out of the car and lit a cigarette. The cemetery was basic, a recent development; had no Gothic-looking statuary, and was essentially a lawn with dividing hedges and headstones. A wide path led to the far end, which was awaiting occupants, and here and there were standpipes where visitors could fill watering cans, with which to tend the plots of their beloveds. Lamb, who carried his dead round with him, didn't spend a lot of time in graveyards. This one didn't seem busy, but perhaps Wednesday afternoons were a slack period.

St. Albans was ringing a bell, though. He sorted through his mental files, and came up with the name Dieter Hess.

Who'd run a ghost network from here, and had now joined one of his own.

Wondering if Hess was nearby, and to give himself time to smoke more, Lamb wandered up the path. The only other human in sight was an elderly woman sitting on a bench, possibly planning ahead. At the far end he counted down a row of newer headstones. Sure enough, third along was Dieter Hess's; a simple stone with just his name and dates. A lot of story crammed between two numbers.

Lamb regarded the stone. A ghost network. The lengths some people go to for a few extra quid, he thought; but knew, too, that the money hadn't been all of it. The reason they called it The Game was that there were always those ready to play, even if that meant switching sides. Ideology, too, was just another excuse.

But now the old boy was buried, and no harm done. At least, Lamb hoped there was no harm done . . . He didn't trust dying messages, and Hess's posthumous list fell under that heading. When something was hidden, but not so well that it couldn't be found, the possibility existed that that had been the intention. And if a ghost network consisted of nine shut-ins and one living breathing young woman, well: a suspicious mind might think that resembled bait.

He dropped his cigarette and ground it underfoot. It was too much of a stretch, he conceded. Would have meant that the hypothetical Hans, far from being Dieter Hess's dupe, was truly cunning: paying Hess simply to hide a coded list under his carpet, knowing that when he pegged out, his flat would be steam-cleaned—when a spy passes, his cupboards need clearing out. So the tenth name would come into the hands of the Service, and maybe—just maybe—its owner, already in the employ of the BND, would be adopted by MI5.

And what looked like a ready-made double would become, in fact, a triple.

But plots need willing players. Lamb could accept that a young woman with a sense of adventure might let herself be recruited by a foreign service in her teens, but didn't think John Bachelor had the nous to play his part, and re-recruit her in turn; or, come to that, that Diana Taverner would give him the green light to do so. Taverner was ambitious, but she wasn't stupid. Too bad for Hans, then. Sometimes you put a lot of effort into schemes that never paid off. Everyone had days like that, though today—thinking of the booty in the boot—wasn't one of Lamb's.

An atavistic impulse had him bend over, find a pebble, and place it on Hess's headstone.

One old spook to another, he thought, then headed back to the car.

Later that same afternoon, Hannah Weiss made her way home by tube. It had been a good day. Her probation at BIS was over; her supervisor had given her two thumbs up, and let her know that great things were expected of her. This could mean anything, of course; that a lifetime of key performance indicators and quarterly assessments lay ahead; or that her career would stretch down Whitehall's corridors, far into an unimaginable distance. "Great things" could mean Cabinet level. It wasn't impossible. She had influential support, after all, even if it had to remain covert. This was the life she had chosen.

She changed at Piccadilly, and found herself standing on a platform next to a middle-aged man in a white raincoat. He carried a rolled-up copy of *Private Eye*. When the train arrived they stepped on board together, and were crammed into a corner of the carriage. The train pulled away, and she found herself leaning against his arm.

For upwards of a minute, the train rattled and lurched through the darkness. And then, just as it began to slow, and the next station hauled into sight, she felt him shift so that his lips were above her ear.

"*Wir sind alle sehr stolz auf dich*, Hannah," he said. Then the train halted, the doors opened, and he was gone.

We're all very proud of you.

A fresh crowd enveloped Hannah Weiss. Deep inside its beating heart, she hugged secret knowledge to herself.

Continue reading for a preview of

NOBODY WALKS

1.1

The news had come hundreds of miles to sit waiting for days in a mislaid phone. And there it lingered like a moth in a box, weightless, and aching for the light.

The street cleaners' lorry woke Bettany. It was 4:25 A.M. He washed at the sink, dressed, turned the bed's thin mattress, and rolled his sleeping bag into a tight package he leaned upright in a corner. 4:32.

Locking the door was an act of faith or satire—the lock would barely withstand a rattle—but the room wouldn't be empty long, because someone else used it during the day. Bettany hadn't met him, but they'd reached an accommodation. The daytime occupant respected Bettany's possessions—his toothbrush, his sleeping bag, the dog-eared copy of *Dubliners* he'd found on a bus—and in return Bettany left untouched the clothing that hung from a hook on the door, three shirts and a pair of khakis.

His own spare clothing he kept in a duffel bag in a locker at the sheds. Passport and wallet he carried in a security belt with his mobile, until that got lost or stolen.

Outside was February cold, quiet enough that he could hear water rinsing the sewers. A bus grumbled past, windows fogged. Bettany nodded to the whore on the corner, whose territory was bounded by two streetlights. She was Senegalese, pre-op, currently a redhead, and he'd bought her a drink one night, God knew why. They had exile in common, but little else. Bettany's French remained undistinguished, and the hooker's English didn't lend itself to small talk.

A taste of the sea hung in the air. This would burn off later, and be replaced by urban flavours.

He caught the next bus, a twenty-minute ride to the top of a lane which fell from the main road like an afterthought, and as he trudged downhill a truck passed, horn blaring, its headlights yellowing the sheds ahead, which were barn-sized constructions behind wire-topped fences. A wooden sign hung lopsided from the gates, one of its tethering chains longer than the other. The words were faded by weather. Bettany had never been able to make them out.

Audible now, the sound of cattle in distress.

He was waved through and fetched his apron from the locker room. A group of men were smoking by the door, and one grunted his name.

"Tonton."

What they called him, for reasons lost in the mist of months.

He knotted his apron, which was stained so thick with blood and grease it felt plastic, and fumbled his gloves on.

Out in the yard the truck was impatient, its exhaust fumes

spoiling out in thick black ropes. The noise from the nearest shed was mechanical, mostly, and its smells metallic and full of fear. Behind Bettany men stamped their cigarettes out and hawked noisily. Refrigerated air whispered from the truck's dropped tailgate.

Bettany's role wasn't complicated. Lorries arrived bearing cattle and the cattle were fed into the sheds. What came out was meat, which was then ferried away in different lorries. Bettany's job, and that of his companions, was to carry the meat to the lorries. This not only required no thought, it demanded thought's absence.

At day's end he'd hose down the yard, a task he performed with grim diligence, meticulously blasting every scrap of matter down the drains.

He switched off, and the working day took over. This was measured in a familiar series of aches and smells and sounds, the same actions repeated with minor variations, while blurred memories nagged him uninvited, moments which had seemed unexceptional at the time, but had persisted. A woman in a café, regarding him with what might have been interest, might have been contempt. An evening at the track with Majeed, who was the nearest he'd made to a friend, though he hadn't made enemies. He didn't think he'd made enemies.

Thoughts became rituals in themselves. You plodded the same course over and over, like any dumb beast or wind-up toy.

At about the time citizens would be leaving their homes in clean shirts Bettany stopped for coffee, pitch black in a polystyrene cup. He ate a hunk of bread wrapped round cheese, leaning against the fence and watching grey weather arrive, heading inland.

From three metres' distance Majeed detached himself from a group similarly occupied.

"Hey, Tonton. You lose your mobile?"

It spun through the air. He caught it one-handed.

"*Ou?*"

"*La Girondelle.*"

The bar at the track. He was surprised to see it again, though the reason why wasn't long in coming.

"*C'est de la merde.* Not worth stealing."

Bettany gave no argument.

The piece of shit, not worth stealing, was barely worth ringing either, though still had a flicker of charge. Four missed calls in nine days. Two were local numbers and hadn't left messages. The others were from England, unfamiliar streams of digits. Odds were they were cold calls, checking out his inclinations vis-à-vis internet banking or double-glazing. He finished his coffee undecided whether to listen or delete, then found his thumb resolving the issue of its own accord, scrolling to his voicemail number, pressing play.

"Yes, this is Detective Sergeant Welles, speaking from Hoxton police station. Er, London. I'm trying to reach a Mr. Thomas Bettany? If you could give me a ring at your earliest convenience. It's a matter of some importance." He recited a number slowly enough that Bettany caught it the first time.

His mouth was dry. The bread, the cheese, grew lumpy in his stomach.

The second voice was less measured.

"Mr. Bettany? Liam's father?" It was a girl, or young woman. "My name's Flea, Felicity Pointer? I'm calling about Liam . . . Mr. Bettany, I'm so sorry to have to tell you this."

She sounded sorry.

"There's been an accident. Liam—I'm sorry, Mr. Bettany. Liam died."

Either she paused a long while or the recorded silence dragged itself out in slow motion, eating up his pre-paid minutes.

"I'm sorry."

"Message ends. To hear the message envelope, press one. To save the—"

He killed the robot voice.

Nearby, Majeed was halfway through a story, dropping into English when French wasn't obscene enough. Bettany could hear the creaking of a trolley's metal wheels, a chain scraping over a beam. Another lorry trundled down the lane, its grille broad, an American model. Already details were stacking up. More blurred snapshots he'd flick through in future days, always associated with the news just heard.

He reached for the back of his neck, and untied his apron.

"Tonton?"

He dropped it to the ground.

"*Ou vas-tu?*"

Bettany fetched his duffel from the locker.

1.2

The crematorium was single-storey, stucco-clad, with a high chimney. On one side creeping plants swarmed a cane trellis that bordered an array of small gardens divided by hedges. Japanese stones neighboured ornamental ponds and bonsai trees peered from terracotta pots. Other patches echoed formal English styles, orchards, terraced rosebeds, in any of which you might strew the ashes of the departed, supposing the deceased had expressed a preference.

Bettany imagined Liam saying, *When I'm dead, scatter me on a Japanese garden. Not in actual Japan. Just anywhere handy.*

A mild English winter was turning chill, but all that remained of the morning's frost was a damp smudge on the pavements. The imprints of vanished leaves were stamped there too, like the work of a graffiti artist who'd run out of things to say.

Bettany's once-blond shaggy hair was now streaked grey, like his ragged beard, and while his eyes were strikingly blue, their expression was vague. His hands, large and raw, were jammed in the pockets of a cheap raincoat, and he rocked slightly on feet cased in work boots that had seen better days. Under the coat he wore jeans, a long-sleeved crew-neck tee and a zippered top. These were the spare clothes from his duffel bag, but three days' wear had taken their toll. The duffel itself he'd abandoned in a bin, he couldn't remember which side of the Channel. For all the hours he'd spent on buses, he'd managed little sleep. His only conversation had been a brief exchange on the ferry, when a French trucker lent him the use of a phone charger.

His first stop on reaching London had been Hoxton Police Station.

Detective Sergeant Welles, once located, had been sympathetic.

"I'm sorry for your loss."

Bettany nodded.

"Nobody seemed to know where you were. But there was an idea you were out of the country. I'm glad you got back in time."

Which was how he discovered the cremation was taking place that morning.

He'd sat in the back row. The chapel of remembrance was quarter-full, most of the congregation Liam's age, none of them known to him, but an introduction contained a familiar name, Felicity Pointer. Flea, she'd called herself on the phone. She approached the lectern looking twenty-five, twenty-six, brunette and lightly olive-skinned, wearing black of course. Hardly looking at the assembled company, she read a short poem about chimney sweeps, then returned to her seat.

Watching this, Bettany had barely paid attention to the main object of interest, but looking at it now he realised that what he'd been feeling these past three days was not grief but numbness. A pair of curtains provided the backdrop, and behind them the coffin would soon pass, and there the remains of his only son would be reduced to ash and fragments of bone, to the mess of clinker you'd find in a grate on a winter's morning. Nothing of substance. And all Bettany could make of it was an all-consuming absence of feeling, as if he was indeed the stranger his son had made of him.

He rose and slipped out of the door.

Waiting by the trellis, it struck him that it was seven years since he'd been in London. He supposed he ought to be noticing differences, things being better or worse, but he couldn't see much had changed. The skyline had altered, with new towers jutting heavenwards from the City, and more poised to sprout everywhere you looked. But that had always been the case. London had never been finished, and never would be. Or not by dint of new construction.

Seven years since London, three of them in Lyme. Then Hannah had died, and he'd left England. Now Liam had died, and he was back.

Welles had given him a lift here. There might have been a hidden agenda, pump the father for information, but Bettany had none to offer and the flow had gone the other way. How it had happened, for instance. Up through France, across the choppy Channel, Bettany hadn't known the how. Of the various possibilities some kind of traffic accident had seemed most likely, Liam driving too fast on a fog-bound stretch of motorway, or a bus mounting the pavement, Liam in the wrong place. He could have called and spared himself conjecture, but that would have been to make imagination fact. Now he learned that there had been no cars involved, no buses. Liam had fallen from the window of his flat.

"Were you in close contact with your son, Mr. Bettany?"

"No."

"So you wouldn't know much about his lifestyle?"

"I don't even know where he lived."

"Not far from here."

Which would make it N1. Not somewhere Bettany was familiar with. He gathered it was trendy, if that word was used any more, and if it wasn't, well then. Cool. Hip. Whatever.

Had Liam been hip? he wondered. Had Liam been cool? They hadn't spoken in four years. He couldn't swear to any aspect of his late son's life, down to the most basic details. Had be been gay? Vegetarian? A biker? What did he do at weekends, browse secondhand shops, looking for bargain furniture? Or hang around the clubs, looking to score? Bettany didn't know. And while he could find out, that wouldn't erase the indelible truth of this particular moment, the one he spent outside the chapel where Liam's body was being fed into the flames. Here and now, he knew nothing. And still, somehow, felt less.

Overhead, a stringy scrap of smoke loosed itself from the chimney. Then another. And now here came the rest of it, billowing and scattering, a cloud for only a moment, and then nothing, and nowhere, ever again.

1.3

The chapel had both entrance and exit, and fresh mourners were congregating at the former. Leaving them, Bettany wandered round to the back, where those who'd come for Liam were dispersing. He was the only blood relative here—there were no others. Liam, an only child, had been the son of only children. And his mother was four years dead.

Loitering under a tree, he watched Flea Pointer emerge. She was talking to an older man, himself flanked by another—flanked, as if the second man were a minder or subordinate. The first man was mid-thirties or so, and while dark suits were the order of the day his seemed of a different cut, the cloth darker, the shirt whiter. A matter of money, Bettany supposed. His short hair was fair to the point of translucence, and his wire-framed glasses tinted blue. As Bettany watched Pointer leaned forward and kissed him on the cheek, her arm curling round his back for a moment, and the man tensed. He raised his hand as if to pat her on the back, but thought better of it. Releasing him, she brushed a palm across her eyes, sweeping her hair free or dabbing at tears. They exchanged inaudible words and the men moved off, down the path, through the gate into the street, and disappeared inside a long silver car, which pulled off with barely a noise. Flea Pointer still hadn't moved.

She was the same age as Liam had been, though unlike Liam was petite—Liam had been a tall boy, gangly, with arms and legs too spindly to know where their centre of balance lay. He'd filled as he'd grown, and had maybe kept doing so. He might have barrelled out since then. Bettany didn't know.

As he stood thinking such things, the girl looked round and saw him.

Flea Pointer watched Vincent Driscoll climb into the limo and pull away, Boo Berryman driving. She had felt him flinch when she put her arm round him—Vincent wasn't much for human contact. She had forgotten that in the emotion of the moment, or else had thought that he might forget it in that same emotion. But he hadn't, so he'd flinched, and she was left feeling gauche and adolescent, as if there weren't enough feelings washing around her now. Tears were not far away. The world threatened to blur.

But she blinked, and it shimmied back. When vision cleared, she was looking at a man standing under a tree like a figure in a fable. He was tall, bearded, shaggy-haired, inappropriately dressed, and she wasn't sure which of these details clinched it, but she knew he was Liam's father. With that knowledge slotted in place, she approached him.

"Mr. Bettany?"

He nodded.

"I'm Flea—"

"I know."

He sounded brusque, but why wouldn't he? His son had just

been cremated. The emotion of the moment, again. She knew this could take different forms.

On the other hand, he'd never responded to her phone call. She'd dug his number out from a form at work, Liam's next-of-kin contact. Couldn't recall exactly what she'd said. But he'd never called back.

What he said now, though, was, "You rang me. Thank you."

"You live abroad."

This sounded disjointed even to her own ears.

"Liam told me," she added.

How else would she have known? She was coming adrift from this exchange already.

"I'm so sorry, I hated to tell you like that, but I didn't know what else to do—"

"You did the right thing."

"I know you hadn't been getting on. I mean, Liam said you didn't—hadn't—"

"We hadn't been in touch," Bettany said.

His gaze left hers to focus on something behind her. Without meaning to, she turned. A small group, three men, one woman, still lingered by the chapel door, but even as she registered this they began to move off. Instead of heading for the gate they walked round to the front, as if heading back inside. One of the men was carrying something. It took Flea a moment to recognise it as a thermos flask.

Liam's father asked her, "Who was that you were talking to?"

"When?"

"He just left."

"Oh . . . That was Vincent. Vincent Driscoll?"

It was clear he didn't know who Vincent Driscoll was.

"We worked for him. Liam and I did. Well, I still do."

She bit her lip. Tenses were awkward, in the company of the bereaved. Apologies had to be implied, for the offence of still living.

"So you were colleagues," he said. "Doing what?"

"Vincent's a game designer. *Shades*?"

Bettany nodded, but she could tell the name meant nothing.

Distantly, music swelled. The next service was starting. Flea Pointer had the sudden understanding that life was a conveyor belt, a slow rolling progress to the dropping-off point, and that once you'd fallen you'd be followed by the next in line. An unhappy thought, which could be shrugged off anywhere but here.

If Tom Bettany was having similar thoughts you wouldn't know it from his expression. He seemed just barely involved in what had happened here this morning.

"Thank you," he said again, and left. Flea watched as he headed down the path.

He didn't look back.

1.4

In the car leaving the crematorium Vincent Driscoll felt one of his headaches coming on, a designation his late mother had coined to distinguish Vincent's headaches from anyone else's. It seemed to fit. There was no denying whose headache this was. It felt like a bubble was squeezing its way through his brain.

He found his Ibuprofen, dry-swallowed a pair, and asked Boo to drive more slowly, or thought he did, and sank back. Had he actually spoken? The world through his tinted glasses, edges softened, passed by at the same speed.

Left to his own devices, he'd have avoided the service. He hated gatherings, and this one had changed nothing. Liam Bettany remained dead. Which was the kind of thing he mostly remembered not to say aloud, but there was no rule he couldn't think it. Probably everyone had thoughts like that, the whole notion of "polite society" being little more than a hedge against honesty. Normality was rarely what it appeared. This much Vincent knew.

And this time, he definitely spoke out loud. "Boo? Could you . . ."

He mimed a movement, a gesture with no obvious correlation to any of the actions involved in driving a car, but which

Boo Berryman, watching in the rearview mirror, interpreted correctly. He slowed down. Vincent closed his eyes.

A succession of pastel-coloured characters drifted past, walking down perfectly straight streets, lined with traditional shops. Each was armed with a shopping list, and carried a basket under an arm, and each popped into every shop in turn, in a perfectly choreographed retail ballet . . . A round yellow sun rose and fell in the sky behind them.

Vincent, who had dreamt up *Shades* when he was twelve, sometimes wondered how many others there were who could ascribe their entire life story to one moment, one striking thought. Einstein, perhaps. Maybe Douglas Adams. Anyway. He'd been playing Tetris, in that semi-catatonic way it induced, when he'd had the sudden sense of things having flipped—that he was the game, not the player.

That had been the spark. Everything else had taken years. But years were what he had had, this being an advantage of having your big idea young.

The car purred to a halt. Traffic lights. Various noises, muffled by thick windows, sprayed past as if fired from a shotgun. Heavy beats and pitched whistling. Sounds of metal and rubber, of the forces that drove everything. If he had ever found a form of music he enjoyed, this was when he would listen to it . . .

Shades had started small, in the sense that it was a one-man show. The team he had now, marketing and packaging and all the rest—he'd had nobody then. Design had happened in his bedroom. Production, outsourced piecemeal to half a dozen tiny companies, had swallowed every penny of his mother's legacy. The result resembled an arcade giveaway, a game fated to be bundled up with others and sold as a lucky dip. Even the small independent he'd hired to mastermind distribution tried to talk him down. The number of titles coming onto the market, if you didn't get traction in the first quarter, you were history. He'd be better off using it on a CV, blagging his way into a job with one of the big boys. But he'd insisted on going ahead.

And it had started small, too, in the sense that not many people bought it. Turned on its head, though—the way Vincent liked to look at things—what this meant was, it was bought only by those who bought everything, which was fine by him. A steady trickle diminishing to a drip, but fine by him. Because, monitoring the comment boards, Vincent knew nobody had cracked it. If that happened and the trickle remained a trickle, he'd know he'd failed. But until then, everyone else had.

Besides, Vincent knew gamers. Gamers were essentially kids, and didn't throw games away. They swapped them and left them gathering dust and stacked them in towers twenty jewelcases high, but they didn't throw them away because that was an adult trait. And games that didn't get thrown away eventually got played again, once they were old enough to have regained novelty value.

The big danger was the format would become extinct, and that had given him a bad night or two, had tempted him to nudge events himself, and post his own message.

But not long after the game's first birthday, everything changed.

Vincent picked it up on a gamers' board.

anyone cracked Shades?

When he'd read this, something shifted inside him.

Home. Sometimes Vincent waited for Boo to open the door, but today he was out of the car before the electronic gates whumped shut. In the kitchen he ran the tap to make sure the water was cold, then filled a glass. This he drained without turning the tap off. He filled a second, and drank that too. Then a third. His headache decreased to a background grumble. He filled a fourth glass and carried it back into the sitting room, which covered most of the ground floor. Boo was just coming in, and flashed him a concerned look. Vincent shook his head, meaning leave him alone. Boo carried straight on into the kitchen, where Vincent heard him turn the tap off. Vincent loosened his tie and sank into a chair.

Above another sofa was a picture, seven foot by four, of a cartoon dog. Some cartoon dogs look intelligent, others dim or violent. Some manage sexy. This one pulled off the relatively simple trick of being nondescript, an expressionless brown mongrel, captured in the act of walking against a two-tone background, the lower half grey, the upper yellow. Those who knew the dog recognised these shades for what they were, which was pavement and wall. And nobody who didn't know the dog had ever seen the picture, so alternative interpretations had never been offered.

follow the dog

That had been the clue offered by that first gamer, the one who'd "cracked" *Shades*. By the time Vincent had revisited the board, it was in meltdown.

holy shit

that is awsum!

way!!!

Shades had been written off by serious gamers, as Vincent had expected. They demanded high-spec graphics, way beyond his budget at the time, and this was just another kitsch time-passer, whose animated figures echoed BBC kids' programming from the '80s, all big heads and fixed smiles, wandering round in a *Truman Show*–like daze, collecting shopping. It was a speed-trial, in which the player had to gather the various items on a list faster than the game-generated characters managed. If you changed the order in which you visited the shops, you could shave seconds off your total, but ran the risk that by the time you got to, say, the butcher's, he'd be out of sausages. There was—so the rules governing such games dictated—a perfect schematic, if the player could only discover it, one which took into account all the other characters' purchases, and the order in which they did things. These days, it might be one of fifty games stored on a phone, something to while away a journey. Even then it was nothing special, a different league from the Lara Crofts, the FPSs.

Nothing special unless you followed the dog.

The dog was a jerky-looking mutt, and if you played the game four times on the trot it appeared briefly on the main street, ambled round a corner and up an alley, and paused halfway to piss on a lamp post. Most players who'd stuck that far had assumed that was it, a little reward for persistence. An animated dog taking a cartoon piss. After which it trotted round another corner and out of sight.

But if, instead of heading into a shop to collect the next item on the list, you followed the dog round that corner, and kept on following it until it dug its way under a bush on a scrappy piece of wasteland which didn't appear to have been there until that moment—because it hadn't, in fact, been there until that moment—and scrabbled down the resulting hole after it, well, once you'd done that, you were in a whole new world.

Raising his glass to his lips, Vincent discovered it empty. He'd drained it without noticing. Still thirsty, though. But perhaps that was unsurprising, given that he'd spent the morning watching a coffin being fed into the flames—which couldn't actually be seen, but was impossible to ignore. The wooden box, with its unnecessarily plush interior, sliding into an oven, never to come out. The smoke drifting into the sky . . . Another gateway, he thought. A chimney instead of a hole, but still, another gateway into a new world.

And Liam Bettany discovering this one now, just as he'd discovered the other.

anyone cracked Shades?

Liam had been the first to follow the dog. In a way Vincent owed him everything, which had never occurred to him until this moment. It wasn't an important thought, but felt similar enough to grief that he savoured it a while—tended it, to see if it would grow—and even when it didn't, held on to it a little longer, carrying it back into the kitchen, where he poured another glass of water while Boo prepared a late lunch.

1.5

The policeman had told him where Liam had lived, a rented third-floor flat, and Bettany had memorised the address but had no idea where it was. He stopped at the first shop he came to and asked the woman behind the counter for help. It wasn't far. She gave efficient directions.

He'd have bought something from her but only had euros, and not many, forty or so. Maybe thirty quid, enough to feed himself at least. He hadn't eaten in how long? Memory suggested a fast-chicken franchise on the ferry, and alongside this image sat another, of oil-flecked water, and big-winged gulls on the watch for spilled food.

The address was one of a terraced row twelve houses long on a quiet street. The row was brick, and the upper windows boasted wrought-iron railings wrapped around ledges no wider than shelves. Greenery sprouted in pots from some, and he could make out a bird feeder on one, small pouches of nuts hanging from its curling branches.

It was accidental. He fell from the balcony, kind of balcony, of his flat.

The windowframes were uniformly white, as if in response to some local mandate, but the doors were vari-coloured, blues, reds, greens and purples. The door of Liam's building was red.

Bettany rang the bell.

The landlord's name was Greenleaf, and the ground floor was where he lived. He was a thin, needy-looking man in plaid shirt and baggy trousers, his eyes set far back in his head. On learning Bettany's name he wrinkled with suspicion, as if Bettany were responsible for the aggravation involved in having a fatal accident on the premises.

"I knew nothing about any of this drug-taking," he said.

"I'd like the key."

"It's in the lease. No illegal substances on the premises."

"Noted. The key?"

"What do you want it for?"

Bettany said, "I'm going to collect my son's possessions. Do you have a problem with that?"

He didn't think he'd leaned on this especially, but Greenleaf stepped back.

"No need to get aggressive."

He left Bettany hanging in the hall while he disappeared behind a door, emerging at length with a key on a string.

"How long will you be?"

There was maybe a joke there, relating to the piece of string, but Bettany couldn't summon up the interest. Without replying, he took the key and carried on up the stairs.

Was he drunk?

He'd been drinking.

Drugs?

We think that's why he was out on the balcony. Kind of balcony.

The top-floor landing was graced with a skylight, through

which grey light fell like drizzle. There was a door on either side. Liam's opened, with his key, onto a small hallway, into which similar light fell from a companion skylight, this one blazoned with a streak of bird shit. The walls were white and the carpet beige, a little scuffed. The air was stale, but Bettany had known worse.

There were three rooms off the hallway. The first was a cupboard-sized bathroom without a bath, just sink, shower and toilet. The cabinet above the sink was mirrored, and Bettany opened it as much to avoid his reflection as out of curiosity about what it held. Which was the usual. Razor, soap, deodorant, a fresh tube of toothpaste. A bottle of bleach sat next to the toilet, tucked behind the loo brush. The shower was clean, with just the odd speck of mould eating into the grouting. A small print on the wall showed a boat bobbing on an unconvincing sea.

Across the hall was the kitchen, which wasn't much bigger but had room for oven, fridge, sink, washing machine, and overhead cupboards neatly filled with essentials. Tins of pulses, bags of rice, flour, jars of sauces. On a white plastic sink-tidy, a single plate had long since dried itself.

Among the postcards stuck to the fridge was a photo of Hannah from before she grew sick. Unthinkingly he pulled it free for a closer look. But it was no riddle awaiting solution. It was an old photograph, that was all.

The fridge obligingly carried on humming, keeping up the good work of chilling Liam's out-of-date milk and slowly perishing vegetables. An array of bowls, sealed with clingfilm, held leftovers he'd never finish. It was all very clean, Bettany thought. All surfaces wiped. Cutlery in its drawer. Pans in their cupboard, graded by size.

Liam had always been careful about his possessions. Very neat in his arrangements.

Detective Sergeant Welles had told him, "There were effects, odds and ends. What he had in his pockets, I mean."

What he had in his pockets when he'd hit the ground.

"You can collect them from the station. Or . . . Where are you staying, can I ask, sir? You've come from abroad, that right?"

Bettany had said, "I'm not sure yet. Where I'm staying."

The other door led into the living room, which would be a nice bright space on a sunny day, with those big windows. A sofa was set against one wall, alongside a nearly full bookcase. On a low table was an electrical contrivance which Bettany guessed was a music system, and a surprisingly small TV set. A rubber plant, scraping the ceiling, lived between the windows, and a small writing desk with a chair occupied a corner. On it was a flat white laptop with the Apple logo.

Another doorway in the far wall presumably led to the bedroom. Bettany checked. Bed, wardrobe and chest of drawers with a mirror propped on top. The bed was made. A small window looked out on the backs of other, similar houses. Below it was a wooden chair, on which lay a folded pair of jeans.

He returned to the sitting room, with its big windows, which didn't quite reach to the floor.

Sort of balcony?

It's just a ledge. A ledge with a railing, meant for putting plants on, so people in upstairs flats can enjoy a bit of garden. What it's not meant for is smoking a joint on. Because there's not much room for being straight, let alone getting high.

The nearest window had a small security lock. Bettany unscrewed it, released the latch, and heaved the window up as high as it would go. The air that blustered in was cold. Down below, a car was inching into a parking space only marginally larger than itself.

Easing himself through, he stepped onto the balcony not meant for getting high on. It was no more than a foot wide, with a terracotta pot on either end, a dead plant in each. Between the two you could stand, if you were careful, leaning on the brickwork for support. It wasn't somewhere you could grow too comfortable, unless, Bettany supposed, you were young and immortal. When you were young, you could fly, or at least bounce. That was the theory, anyway.

He checked the pot to his left, then made a similar examination of the one on his right. Neither had been used as an ashtray.

This was a pretty strong blend. There's a lot of it around lately. They're calling it muskrat. Well, they'd already used skunk.

Muskrat. Bettany closed his eyes, and imagined the seamless sequence, Liam rolling up, stepping through the window, lighting a joint, and then—what? Losing his balance? Closing his eyes, forgetting where he was? It must have been strong stuff all right. First you get high. Then you come crashing down.

After giving that a little more thought, he climbed back inside.

1.6

Pulling the window shut, Bettany noticed he still held Hannah's photograph. He took it back to the kitchen and reclamped it to the fridge, then had to lean against the wall while a wave of tiredness struck. He needed coffee. Shouldn't be too difficult to manage.

A cafetière sat by the kettle and there was coffee in the fridge. Bettany boiled the kettle, and while the coffee drew, went through cupboards again. Tins, bags of rice and jars of spices. A memory was stirring, but it wasn't until he saw the matching plastic containers marked TEA, BISCUITS, SUGAR that he knew what it was. Reaching for the third container he unscrewed its lid. It held sugar, sure enough, but when he dipped his fingers through its temporary glaze they met a polythene bag, the kind banks use for change, rolled into a tight cylinder. Unwrapping it, Bettany counted out two hundred and forty pounds in twenties.

He weighed it in his hand. The sugar tin was where Hannah had hidden small sums of cash. Bettany used to shake his head—the sugar tin? Please. But that's where she'd kept her emergency fund, and where Liam had kept his too. Bettany shook his head again, less at the way things were handed down, and more at the fact that the police hadn't found it.

They must have been through the flat looking for drugs, if nothing else. Muskrat. Who thought up these names?

The coffee was ready. He poured a cup, left it black, carried it into the sitting room. Taking his raincoat off at last, he draped it over the sofa, then opened Liam's laptop. It swam into life without complaint but asked for a password. After pondering this for a while, Bettany closed the lid.

A yawn caught him unawares. He hadn't slept in—he couldn't bring himself to perform the calculation. Too many hours. He hadn't slept in too many hours. The coffee would help.

When the phone rang he at first didn't realise it was his own, and once he had it took him a moment to locate it. It was in his raincoat pocket, and before he'd retrieved it, the ringing stopped. But in moving the coat, or else putting his weight on the sofa's cushions, he'd released an aroma that hadn't been there before. It wasn't much, a fading scent, but it caught him where he lived, raising hairs at the back of his neck. It was the smell of his son. The ordinary, living smell of Liam, of his soap, and his sweat, and of oils that had seeped from his hair as he sat here, head against the cushions.

The phone rang again.

"Mr. Bettany?"

He didn't reply.

"Mr.—?"

"Yes."

"It's DS Welles, sir. You're at your son's flat, are you?"

"Yes."

"I have his things. His effects."

Effects was a policeman's word.

"And I'm just outside. Should I—"

"I'll come down."

He waited two minutes, then did so. Welles was on the step, offering a brown envelope that might have come from the Revenue, or anywhere else that issued impersonal demands. Bettany took it in his left hand. His right was jammed in his pocket.

"Thanks."

"Are you going to be all right?"

"I expect so."

"Is there anyone—"

"I'll be all right."

"Of course. Here, I need you to sign this, sir."

Bettany scrawled his name on the proffered form, *I hereby acknowledge receipt*, and turned back inside. Before shutting the door he said, "How did you know I was here?"

"Couldn't think where else you'd be."

Upstairs, he turned the envelope over. Objects inside it slipped from side to side. Eventually he ripped the seal and poured its contents onto the table.

A wallet, holding a little over thirty pounds, two credit cards, a supermarket loyalty card and a library ticket.

A set of doorkeys.

A chapstick.

A packet of tissues.

That was it.

He dumped everything on the desk next to the laptop and finished his coffee. Knowing it wasn't a great idea, that it would give him the jitters, he poured a second cup anyway, drained it, and poured a third. That was the end of the coffee. He wandered the flat again, cup in hand. Everywhere was clean lines, clutter-free surfaces. A thin layer of dust was forming, exactly measurable, Bettany thought, to the day of his son's death. There were no candles melting into wax-smeared holders, no knick-knacks acquired on holiday to forever take up space. No photographs, other than those on the fridge.

None of which were of Bettany.

He wouldn't have expected any. He was surprised Liam had listed his number as an emergency contact—wouldn't have been shocked to learn he was passing as an orphan. As Bettany recalled it, that had been the import of their last conversation.

It's your fault she's dead.

It's cancer's fault, Liam.

And why do you think people get cancer? You made her unhappy. You were a bastard to her, and to me.

There was a whole deluded industry dedicated to the notion that cancer fattened on the emotions, and not for a moment had Bettany believed his son had fallen prey to it. It had been a weapon, that's all. A stick to beat him with.

Had he been a bastard? He'd been called worse.

One of the pictures of Liam was recent, taken indoors. His hair, always darker than his father's, was cut short, and he wore a white collarless shirt, open at the neck. Half-smiling, half-serious, he seemed to be trying to impress the photographer with both sides of his personality. Twenty-six years old. Bettany unclipped it and carried it into the other room.

On the sofa he closed his eyes, photo on his chest. It was quiet. Caffeinated to the eyeballs, he didn't expect to sleep but drifted anyway, memories of a much younger Liam overlapping with those of Hannah, distant snapshots that offered no clue to how badly things would go awry. *It's your fault she's dead.* There was no way in the world those words were true, and no way to unremember them.

The light through the windows had weakened when he stood and put his raincoat on. Leaving the flat, he went downstairs. When Greenleaf opened the door he was holding a paper napkin, wiping his mouth. He'd missed a fleck of grease that shone on his chin.

"Did you bring the key back?" he said.

"When was the rent paid up to?"

"I can't remember offhand." Greenleaf's eyes glazed, as if he were engaged in a mental calculation he'd hoped would be overlooked. "I could work it out, refund the balance. Leave your address and I'll post you a cheque."

"No need," Bettany said. "I'll be upstairs. Until the rent's used up."

He didn't wait for a response. Outside, he stood for a while by the patch of road where Liam's life had ended. Nothing distinguished that space from any other. It was just where something had happened. Looking up at the building offered no stories either. Everything carried on doing what it had always done. Bettany put his hands in his pockets, and went walking.

1.7

Flea Pointer had a problem, a problem the size of a box, which was precisely what it was. Inside the box was an urn, squatter and rounder than she might have imagined, and inside the urn was Liam Bettany.

In life, Liam had been tall, limby—not a real word but his limbs had been noticeably long, his hands dangling lower than seemed plausible, his legs an obstacle in the workplace. As days wore on he'd sink lower and lower into his chair, allowing them to protrude further and further, and more than once, passing his desk, she'd nearly gone flat on her face. His response was always an apologetic grin.

She'd never really tripped, though. Never fallen.

Flea was in her studio flat in a canalside development near the Angel. Better apartments had more rooms and overlooked the lock, but Flea wasn't complaining. Before this there'd been a series of house shares, most of which had degenerated into attritional warfare, the battlegrounds being bathroom and kitchen, and whose stuff was whose. She'd seen violence break out over a pint of milk. Now, when the walls felt like they were closing in, she heaved a sigh of relief they were closing on her alone.

Not quite alone at the moment, though. Liam was here too.

Her colleagues had taken off to a pub once the service was over, and were presumably still there, toasting Liam and celebrating small memories of him, like her own recollection of his troublesome legs. She had joined them for an hour before returning to the crem to take possession of the ashes, which she'd half-expected Vincent to do, though on reflection wasn't sure why. Vincent had taken care of expenses, but he'd never realistically been likely to step higher than that. So here she was, and here Liam was too, in a box on her table, her friend.

There'd been a time when they might have been more than friends, but in the end—or before the beginning—Flea had decided this was a bad idea. So now, instead of memories of a romantic interlude, she was left thinking about his long legs, and how they stuck out too far, and could easily have caused an accident.

Which evidently they had done, if not to her. She knew that ledge outside his window, with its low railing that came halfway up his calves. No wonder he'd gone over. If she'd been with him last week—and it wouldn't have been the first time they'd sat out there together, getting high—she might have saved him.

On the other hand she might have been left sitting stoned on the balcony, looking down at his body, knowing her life was as irrevocably twisted, as bent out of shape, as he was . . .

Flea Pointer shook her head. Dreadful imaginings. And utterly selfish at their root, which she didn't mean to be, not today. Not with Liam gone.

She'd miss his grin.

She cried again.

■   ■   ■

Afterwards, tears dry, the problem endured. Liam's ashes remained on her coffee table, and fond as she'd been of him she didn't want him as a roommate, even if arguments about the milk weren't likely to arise.

The answer, of course, was staring her in the face. It was simply a matter of deciding whether it meant being disloyal to Liam.

Seeing Tom Bettany at the service had been a surprise. Because he hadn't responded she'd assumed he'd not received her message, or had no intention of acting on it. Liam would have professed to believe the latter. When in full flow about his father—a man he insisted he didn't like talking about—he'd revealed more than he intended, but given that on such occasions he was usually a little drunk or a little high, this was not unusual. Given that Flea too had tended to be one or the other, she couldn't pretend total recall. But they hadn't got on, that was an understatement. Liam had coloured their estrangement in Shakespearean terms, once claiming his father had killed his mother. That moment Flea did recall clearly, along with its pale-faced aftermath, when Liam threw up, luckily in the bathroom, then shakily admitted he'd exaggerated, that it hadn't been an actual killing so much as . . .

And she remembered that too. The way he'd lacked words to state the case. Because, she suspected, when it came down to it, he'd been a boy who'd lost his mother too young, and needed someone to blame. His father fit the bill, that was all.

The murder claim, like others he'd made, Flea put down to immaturity. And the fact that his father's number was on his contact list at work indicated that at some level he'd known it too. Had understood there'd come a time when a bridge would need rebuilding.

Too late for that now.

Still grieving, still pained, Flea couldn't deny she was also curious. Though she'd had no mental picture of Liam's father, it nevertheless surprised her that he resembled a tramp, with shaggy hair and scarecrow's beard, and clothes he'd been wearing a while. And, too, the wariness she'd noticed in homeless people. The way he'd checked out the crowd at the chapel, as if weighing potential threat. But he remained Liam's father, the rightful owner of his son's remains. Presenting him with them wouldn't be an act of disloyalty to Liam but the opposite. And as much of a bridge as either could now hope for.

The solution, then, was a phone call away, but still Flea Pointer hesitated. She had no idea where Bettany was. Perhaps he'd already made tracks, was already standing at a motorway slip road, thumb in the air . . . She didn't know why that image came to mind. He didn't look the type to ask favours of strangers. Which meant he wouldn't want them done unawares, she decided, and that conclusion reached, she looked for her mobile. Do it now. Do it now, and it was done. Her phone was in her bag. She made the call before second thoughts could persuade her otherwise.

Other Titles in the Soho Crime Series